Office Gods

tapas original

Catharina Octorina

Art by Hiikariin

300 YEARS AGO, THEY CAME TO US DURING "THE REVEAL."

THE GODS AND GODDESSES OF MYTH ARE REAL, AND THEY SHOWED THEMSELVES TO HUMANITY TO REMIND US OF THAT.

WE BEGAN LIVING WITH THEM SIDE BY SIDE,

AND THEY BECAME A PERMANENT PRESENCE IN OUR WORLD...

BY ESTABLISHING THE COMPANY "OLYMPUS!"
OLYMPUS IS LOCATED IN A 1000-STORY OFFICE THAT SERVES AS A HUB FOR GODS AND HUMANS.
THROUGH OLYMPUS, THE GODS WERE ABLE TO INTEGRATE INTO HUMAN SOCIETY AND ADAPT TO THE HUMAN WAYS OF OPERATING.
IT WASN'T LONG BEFORE OLYMPUS BECAME THE CORPORATE HEADQUARTERS FROM WHICH THE GODS RAN THE WORLD.
IT'S ALSO WHERE WE HUMANS GO TO GIVE OUR OFFERINGS AND ASK FOR BLESSINGS...
AND WHERE MEETINGS ARE HELD BETWEEN HIGH-STATUS HUMANS AND GODS TO DISCUSS WORLD AFFAIRS.

NATURALLY, OLYMPUS HAS BECOME THE MOST PRESTIGIOUS COMPANY TO WORK FOR IN THE WORLD!

AND TODAY...

TAP

UUGH... SO TIGHT!
THIS SHOULD BE GOOD, RIGHT?

MY FIRST DAY OF WORK AFTER A FULL YEAR OF REJECTIONS FROM ALL SORTS OF COMPANIES...
REJECTION LETTER
REJECTION LETTER
REJECTED
REJECTED
AND SOMEHOW, I GOT ACCEPTED TO OLYMPUS, OF ALL PLACES!

THIS PLACE IS NOTORIOUSLY ELITIST. USUALLY THEY ONLY ACCEPT DEMIGODS OR EXTRA-EXCEPTIONAL HUMANS.
ANYONE WOULD BE NERVOUS ON THEIR FIRST DAY OF WORK, BUT THIS IS ON ANOTHER LEVEL.

BUT NOT EVERYONE GETS AN OPPORTUNITY LIKE THIS, SO I CAN'T LET IT GO TO WASTE!
AND AFTER ALL, THEY CHOSE TO HIRE ME FOR A REASON!
I WONDER WHAT THEY SAW IN ME.
THE EMPLOYEES HERE ARE MOSTLY DEMI-GODS, SO THEY'RE EXCEPTIONALLY BEAUTIFUL...
OF COURSE, SINCE ONE OF THEIR PARENTS IS A GOD, THEY'RE BORN WI MORE BLESSINGS THAN REGULAR HUMANS.
THEY TAKE FEWER SICK DAYS AND WORK MORE EFFICIENTLY, SO THEY'RE NATURALLY MORE VALUED AS EMPLOYEES.
IT'S HARD FOR HUMANS TO COMPETE!

Should I wear more makeup?
BUT HERE I AM!
I DON'T THINK I'M TOO BAD, BUT COMPARED TO THESE BEAUTIES, I FEEL SO OUT OF PLACE...
351
AH! HERE'S MY DEPARTMENT!
AND NOW, I JUST HAVE TO GO IN THERE AND MAKE A GREAT FIRST IMPRESSION--
CLICK
ARE YOU MOCKING ME, ORION?!
I...I THINK I CAME IN AT THE WRONG TIME...
IT LOOKS LIKE TWO IMPORTANT DEMIGODS ARE IN THE MIDDLE OF A FIGHT...
YOU'RE AN ARROGANT PRICK!
BORK
BORK

WHY DID YOU RECOMMEND ME TO ATHENA FOR THE VP POSITION?
YOU THINK I'M NOT CAPABLE OF BECOMING VP ON MY OWN?!
I JUST THOUGHT THAT YOU WANTED THE POSITION MORE THAN ME,
DANTE.

OUR NEW VP IS SO EASY TO ANGER!
They're both so attractive, though...
YEAH, ESPECIALLY WHEN IT COMES TO ORION...

DON'T GIVE ME THAT BULLSHIT!!!
SLAM

!
HUH?

DON'T GIVE ME
HAT BULLSHIT!!!
TUPID HUMAN!!!

WAIT A MINUTE...
WHY DOES HIS VOICE SOUND SO FAMILIAR?
YOU'RE NOT IN YOUR RIGHT MIND...
DANTE, PLEASE...
I... RECOGNIZE THIS VOICE, TOO...

LAST FRIDAY...
BADABOOM
HIS VOICE WAS KIND BUT STERN...
MISS, PLEASE, YOU'RE NOT IN YOUR RIGHT MIND...
AND I WAS SO DRUNK AND STUPID!!!
YOU DON'T UNDERSTAND!
YOU'VE BEEN SO KIND TO ME...
TUG
IT'D BE EASY FOR YOU, RIGHT?
TO COME UPSTAIRS TO MY PLACE.

IT'S THE GUY FROM THE BAR!!!

TAK

I...I NEVER THOUGHT THAT I'D HAVE TO RELIVE THAT NIGHTMARE!
BOTH OF THEM!!!
THE SCARY GUY THAT I PROVOKED...
POUR
DO YOU KNOW HOW MUCH THESE PANTS COST, YOU STUPID HUMAN?!
Y-YOU...
YELL MORE, DEMIGOD.
Splash
AND THE POLITE GUY I DRUNKENLY TRIED TO SEDUCE...!

NO, THANK YOU.

GODS, PLEASE...

SHE FAINTED!
THE NEW GIRL FAINTED!
WHY ARE YOU BEING SO CRUEL TO ME?!

LAST FRIDAY
OF COURSE I'VE ALWAYS KNOWN THIS DAY WOULD COME.
KYO AND I HAVE BEEN BEST FRIENDS SINCE WE LEARNED TO TALK
AND HE WAS THE FIRST AND ONLY GUY I'VE EVER LIKED.
BOTH OF US STAYED SINGLE UNTIL OUR TWENTIES, SO I THOUGHT I HAD A CHANCE WITH HIM.
FULL
GEAR

BUT I SHOULD'VE KNOWN...
AND NOW, THE DAY HAS COME FOR ME TO MEET MY ONLY CRUSH'S GIRLFRIEND!

KYO...
get it together!
HERE, IRIS!

THIS IS IRIS, SHE'S MY NEIGHBOR.
IRIS, MEET ROSE.
ALRIGHT, HERE IT GO--
GLITTERING HAIR...
EYES THAT SHINE LIKE GEMSTONES...
HI, IRIS! NICE TO MEET YOU TOO!
EFFORTLESSLY CHIC
N-NICE TO MEET YOU...
THE WORLD JUST LOVES TO PLAY JOKES ON ME, DOESN'T IT?

SHE'S THE DEMIGODDESS VERSION OF ME!!!

DID YOU KNOW THAT ROSE WORKS AT THAT CELADRON COMPANY?
AH, IT'S NOTHING SPECIAL!
CELADRON... I GOT REJECTED BY THAT COMPANY.
SO, HAVE YOU AND IRIS KNOWN EACH OTHER LONG?
SHE'S LIKE MY SISTER!
I CAN ACCEPT KYO GETTING A GIRLFRIEND, BUT MY POOR HEART ALSO NEEDS A BREAK!

Neon Lights Bar
DISCERNIBLE TALENTS,
AND ON TOP OF THAT, NO JOB.
I'M ONLY 23, BUT I CAN ALREADY TELL THAT MY LIFE IS GOING TO BE A SERIES OF FAILURES...
AND THAT'S WHY YOU CALLED ME HERE, IRIS?
I NEED MORAL SUPPORT, LILY!
COME ON, IRIS. IT'S NOT THAT BAD.
AFTER ALL, YOU DID HAVE AN INTERVIEW WITH THE ESTEEMED OLYMPUS!
EVEN I DIDN'T GET THAT INTERVIEW, AND YOU KNOW HOW MUC I WANTED TO WORK AT OLYMPUS!

I THINK I BOTCHED THAT...
AND I'M PRETTY SURE OLYMPUS IS GONNA HIRE A DEMIGOD INSTEAD OF ME, JUST LIKE THE OTHER COMPANIES.
MAYBE I SHOULD JUST BECOME A COMEDIAN, BECAUSE I'M STARTING TO FEEL LIKE A JOKE.
AAAAH! NONSENSE!
WE'RE TALENTED, BEAUTIFUL WOMEN, BURSTING WITH LIFE! COMPANIES AND BOYS SHOULD LINE UP TO GET A PIECE OF US!
LET'S DRINK AND REMIND OURSELVES OF OUR GREATNESS, IRIS!
YEAH!
ANOTHER BOTTLE, PLEASE!

WE NEED TWO MORE BOTTLES!
WE MAY NOT MATCH DEMIGODS IN TERMS OF BEAUTY, INTELLECT, HEALTH, AND EVEN LIFESPAN...
BUT WE CAN DEFINITELY CRUSH THEM IN ANY DRINKING GAME!
NOTE: THEY WOULD NOT.

IRIS...
LOOK AT THAT GROUP THAT JUST CAME IN...
WHAT A BUNCH OF HOTTIES!

THEY ALL HAVE LUMINOUS SKIN AND STATUESQUE FIGURES!
THEY ALL LOOK LIKE MODELS AND YET, THEY'RE HERE IN THIS BAR WEARING BUSINESS ATTIRE.
THEY MUST BE A GROUP OF DEMIGOD WORKERS, ENJOYING AFTER-OFFICE HOURS...
oh, right! HEY, IRIS!
MAYBE YOU SHOULD FIND YOUR OWN DEMIGOD BOYFRIEND! I MEAN, KYO FOUND HIS--
PBBBLTH
ARE YOU OUT OF YOUR MIND, LILY?
I MEAN, LOOK AT ME!
AND LOOK AT THEM!
WHAP

W-WAIT...
W-WHERE EXACTLY DID MY HAND GO?!
CARELESS HUMAN.
I'M SORRY. I'M REALLY SORRY!
I DIDN'T MEAN TO SLAP YOU TH-THERE!
I CAN'T BELIEVE THAT THE FIRST TIME I TOUCHED A GUY IN THAT AREA IS WHEN I'M DRUNK OUT OF MY MIND LIKE THIS!!!
WHAT A SAD LIFE!!!

THAT'S OKAY. I EXPECT HUMANS TO BE CARELESS AND CLUMSY.
GETTING DRUNK IN PUBLIC AND THEN MAKING A FOOL OUT OF THEMSELVES...
I EXPECTED NOTHING MORE.
HEY, WHAT THE HELL, DUDE! COME BACK HERE AND APOLOGIZE TO MY FRIEND!
HOLD ME BACK, IRIS!
DON'T LET ME HIT HIM!
...IRIS?

W-WHAT ARE YOU DOING?
IRIS!!!

HEY.

IT'S EXPECTED FOR ME TO ACT SLOPPY, HUH?

WHAT THE HELL?

REJECTION LETTER
REJECTED
REJECTED
I'M JUST A PATHETIC HUMAN, RIGHT?
THEN WHO AM I TO DISAPPOINT YOU, MISTER DEMIGOD?

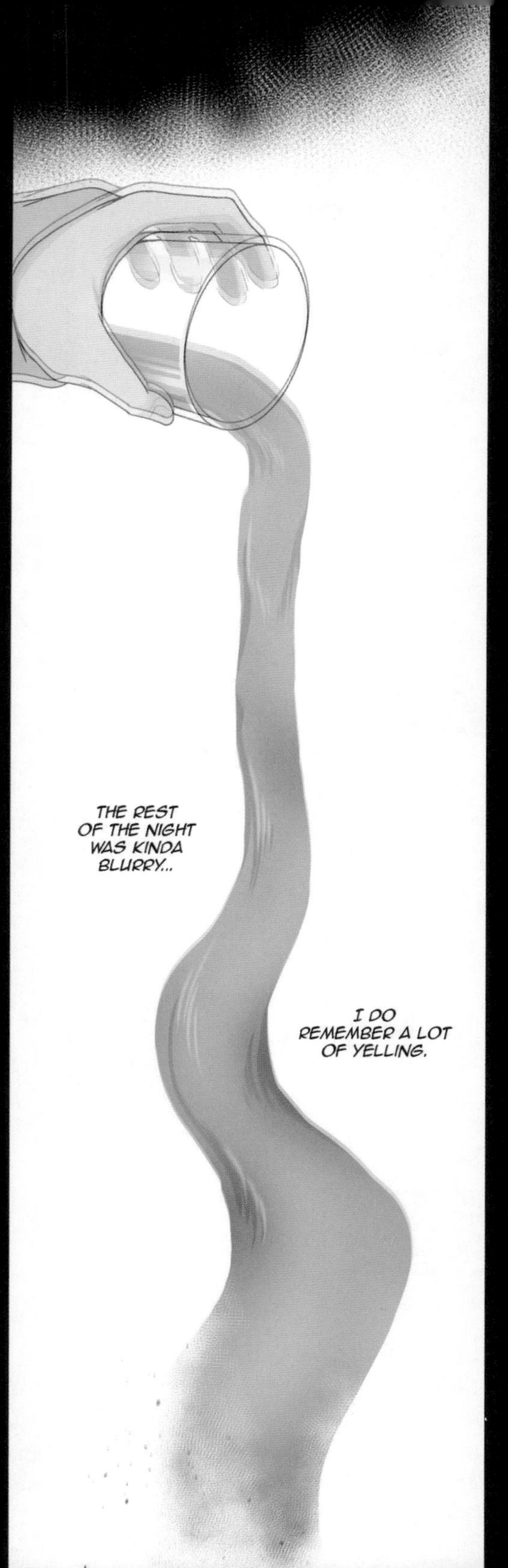
THE REST OF THE NIGHT WAS KINDA BLURRY...
I DO REMEMBER A LOT OF YELLING.

I REMEMBER HOW THE GENTLE-FACED DEMIGOD STOOD BETWEEN ME AND THE ANGRY ONE.
LET IT GO, DANTE.
CAN'T YOU SEE SHE'S NOT IN HER RIGHT MIND?

I REMEMBER
GETTING INTO A TAXI
WITH HIM...

AND THEN I
REMEMBER...

YOU'RE
DRUNK.
NO,
THANK YOU.

THE MOST HUMILIATING MOMENT IN MY LIFE!!!

YOU'VE WOKEN UP.
THAT'S GOOD.

LET ME TAKE YOUR PULSE. YOU WERE BREAKING OUT IN A COLD SWEAT.

HOHOHO!!!
Have I not been subjected to enough for today?

WELL, ORION! FLIRTING WITH MY NEW RECRUIT ON HER FIRST DAY, HUH?
Sir, you're being very loud.
YOU DO HAVE A MYSTERIOUS WAY WITH WOMEN!

WELL, WELL, WELL, ORION, WHAT'S THE MEANING OF THIS?
HERMES...
HERMES? THAT MEANS... MY BOSS?
WHEN IS THIS SUFFERING GONNA END?!

SO, IRIS...
THE OLD MAN HERE IS HERMES, HEAD OF THE COMMUNICATIONS DEPARTMENT. I'M SHIRA, YOUR DIRECT SUPERVISOR.
FROM NOW ON, YOU'LL BE WORKING WITH US.
SHE'S NOT THE HEAD OF ANYTHING BUT LISTEN TO THE WAY SHE TALKS!
YOU'D THINK SHE WAS MY BOSS, RIGHT?
please don't touch me
ouch
AH...NICE TO MEET YOU BOTH!
I-I'M SORRY FOR BEING LATE ON MY FIRST DAY... I WAS--
YOU FAINTED AT THE SIGHT OF THIS GUY, DIDN'T YOU?
DON'T WORRY, YOU'RE NOT THE FIRST HUMAN WHO'S LOST CONSCIOUSNESS WHEN FACED WITH SUCH BEAUTY.
hand. Please.
classic
Y-YOU'RE NOT WRONG, BUT...
HIS FACE IS NOT THE REASON!!!

THERE'S NO USE TRYING TO EXPLAIN EVERYTHING THAT HAPPENED LAST WEEK.
I SHOULD JUST FOCUS ON GETTING MY WORK DONE.
SHIRA, HERMES...
I'M VERY SORRY FOR THE SETBACK THIS MORNING, BUT DON'T WORRY ABOUT ME NOW BECAUSE I'M READY TO WORK.
whistle
SO THIS HUMAN IS QUITE DETERMINED, HUH.
ALRIGHT. GO TAKE HER TO THE OFFICE, SHIRA.
I NEED TO MEET MY COLLEAGUES FOR A VERY IMPORTANT MEETING.
YOU MEAN, YOU WANT TO GOSSIP?
IT'S "GATHERING INTEL FOR THE SAKE OF OUR ESTEEMED MAGAZINE," SHIRA. TSK. GET YOUR FACTS RIGHT.
tsk
tsk
CIAO, THEN. REPORT BACK TO ME ON HOW THE NEWBIE FITS IN.

I NEED TO GO, TOO. NICE TO MEET YOU, IRIS.
YOUR PULSE IS FINE, MAYBE A LITTLE FAST. TRY TO RELAX AND DRINK MORE TEA.
SURE... UH...THANKS, ORION.
WOW, NOW THAT I LOOK AT HIM WHEN I'M SOBER, HE REALLY IS COMPOSED.
IT FEELS WEIRD SAYING HIS NAME!!!

SEE YOU LATER. YOU TOO, SHIRA.
click

YOU THINK HE'S COOL AND HANDSOME, DON'T YOU?
W-WHAT? I MEAN, OBJECTIVELY ANYONE WOULD CALL HIM GOOD-LOOKING, BUT I DIDN'T...
DON'T EVEN BOTHER, NEW KID.
ORION DOESN'T DATE. MOREOVER, HE WILL GO OUT OF HIS WAY TO AVOID DATING A HUMAN.

did that come out too harsh?
?
hmm
ANYWAY, THAT WAS JUST A FRIENDLY PRECAUTION FROM ME TO YOU, MY SUPPOSED JUNIOR.
I am a good, approachable senior
this is approachable?
THANK YOU... FOR THE PRECAUTION...
420
ding
YOU'LL BE WORKING ON THE 420TH FLOOR.

THERE ARE 1000 FLOORS IN OLYMPUS.
SOMETIMES, WE DO MORNING BRIEFINGS ON THE 310TH FLOOR AKA THE GROUND FLOOR, LIKE WE DID THIS MORNING.
AH, I SEE.
YOUR JOB, HOWEVER, MIGHT REQUIRE YOU TO MOVE AROUND A BIT. THOUGH FOR YOU, THE SITUATIONS CAN GET TRICKY.

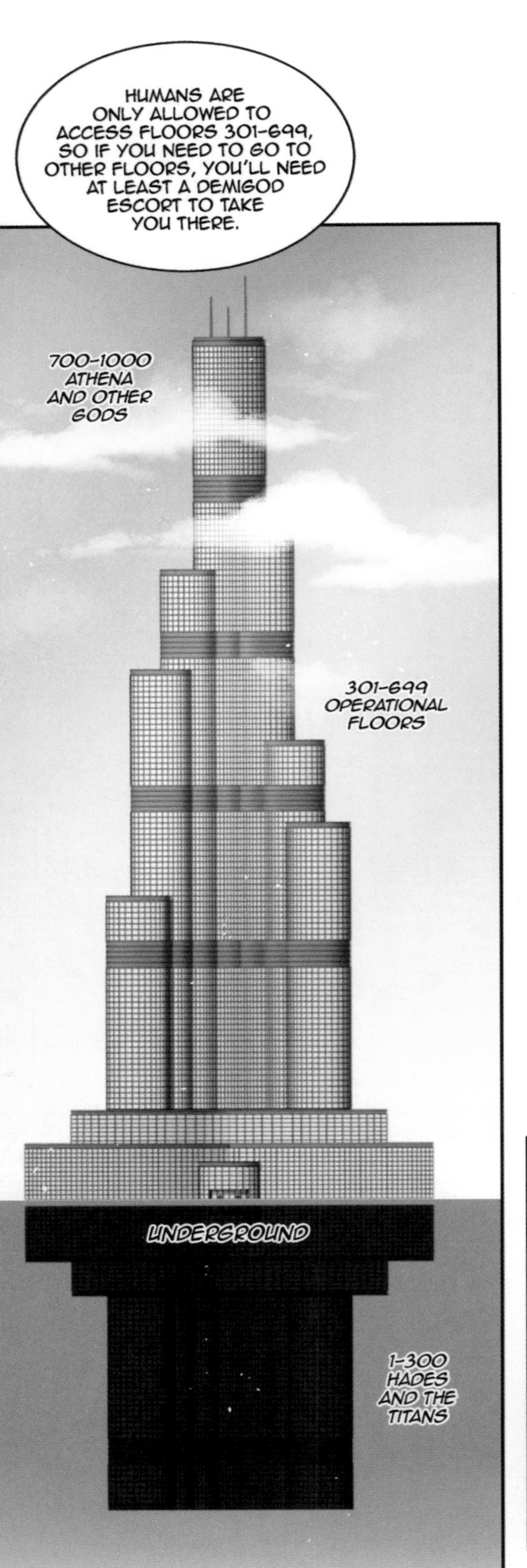
HUMANS ARE ONLY ALLOWED TO ACCESS FLOORS 301-699, SO IF YOU NEED TO GO TO OTHER FLOORS, YOU'LL NEED AT LEAST A DEMIGOD ESCORT TO TAKE YOU THERE.
700-1000 ATHENA AND OTHER GODS
301-699 OPERATIONAL FLOORS
UNDERGROUND
1-300 HADES AND THE TITANS

REALLY?
WHY ARE THOSE FLOORS RESTRICTED FOR HUMANS?

BECAUSE THOSE FLOORS ARE ALSO THE GODS' RESTING PLACES

AND THEY DON'T LIKE GETTING HUMAN VISITORS OUTSIDE OF THE OPERATIONAL OFFICES AREA.
huh?

D-DOES THAT MEAN YOU'LL HELP ME GET AROUND?
OF COURSE NOT. YOU'LL FIGURE IT OUT YOURSELF.
RIGHT...

I MEAN...

YOU GOT IN HERE BECAUSE YOU'RE **SMART** AND **RESOURCEFUL,** RIGHT? YOU SHOULD BE ABLE TO FIGURE OUT HOW TO DO YOUR JOB.

SHIRA'S RIGHT! I NEED TO REMEMBER WHY I'M HERE IN THE FIRST PLACE.
THE BEST COMPANY IN THE WORLD ACCEPTED ME EVEN THOUGH I'M NOT A DEMIGOD OR A NOBEL PRIZE-CANDIDATE HUMAN.
I NEED TO PROVE TO THEM THAT THEY HAVEN'T MADE A MISTAKE. THAT MY PRESENCE HERE ISN'T A BLUNDER ON THEIR PART.
WELCOME TO OUR LITTLE OFFICE, MAILROOM GIRL.

EMPTY
MAILROOM GIRL? I THOUGHT MY JOB WAS "ACCOUNT MANAGER OF INTERDEITIES COMMUNICATIONS"?
calling me 'mailroom girl' is a little--
THAT HERMES IS A FAN OF GIVING EMBARRASSINGLY INFLATED TITLES TO HIS SUBORDINATES...
mine is called 'the highest manager of the communications of the 420th floor'

SORRY. AHEM, YES. YOUR JOB IS TO BE THE MAILROOM GIRL, AKA TO DELIVER MAIL TO VARIOUS GODS.
cough cough

SO HERMES, THE TRICKSTER GOD, REALLY FOOLED BOTH OF US...

YOU SEE ALL THESE CABINETS, IRIS?
THERE'S ABOUT 500 YEARS WORTH OF LETTERS STORED IN THEM.
THEY WERE MOSTLY WRITTEN BY GODS TO OTHER GODS BEFORE WE DISCOVERED TECHNOLOGY.
YOU MEAN, BEFORE HUMANS DISCOVERED TECHNOLOGY...

ANYWAY, THAT'S A LOT OF UNSENT LETTERS.
WHY DON'T THEY JUST TALK TO ONE ANOTHER? MOST OF THEM RESIDE HERE, TOO, RIGHT?
IT'S NOT THAT SIMPLE.
THE GODS ALL HAVE VERY BIG EG-- I MEAN, THEY ARE ALL SHORT ON TIME, AND THEY'RE VERY BUSY KEEPING THE BALANCE IN THE WORLD.
SO, THEY WRITE LETTERS IF THE MATTER IS NOT SO URGENT.

UNFORTUNATELY, DUE TO LACK OF MANPOWER TO DELIVER THESE LETTERS, THEY'VE JUST BEEN PILING UP HERE, IN HERMES' DEPARTMENT.
IT'S EATING UP ALL THE SPACE IN MY OFFICE, SO I ASKED HERMES TO DO SOMETHING ABOUT IT.
THIS ONE WAS DATED FROM 150 YEARS AGO...
THIS ONE IS MORE RECENT, FROM 44 YEARS AGO...
SHIRA... IS THIS ALL MY JOB IS GONNA BE?

YES.
THOSE DARN GODS...SO THEY HIRED ME TO DO THE MOST MENIAL JOB NO ONE WANTS TO TAKE, HUH?!
shuffle
I'LL SHOW THEM!!! I'LL DELIVER ALL THE LETTERS YOU'RE ALL TOO PROUD TO SEND YOURSELVES!
I'LL MAKE THEM HAVE NO CHOICE BUT TO GIVE ME MORE CHALLENGING WORK TO DO!
IT'S PRETTY ODD, THOUGH... TO HIRE A HUMAN TO WORK IN THIS--
swift
swift
swift
shuffle
TA-DA!
I'M OFF, THEN. I'LL BE DELIVERING THESE!

THIS IS YOUR FIRST DAY, SO SHOULD I SHOW YOU THE WAY?
I'LL FIGURE IT OUT!
THANKS FOR THE BRIEF, SHIRA. I'LL COME BACK LATE--

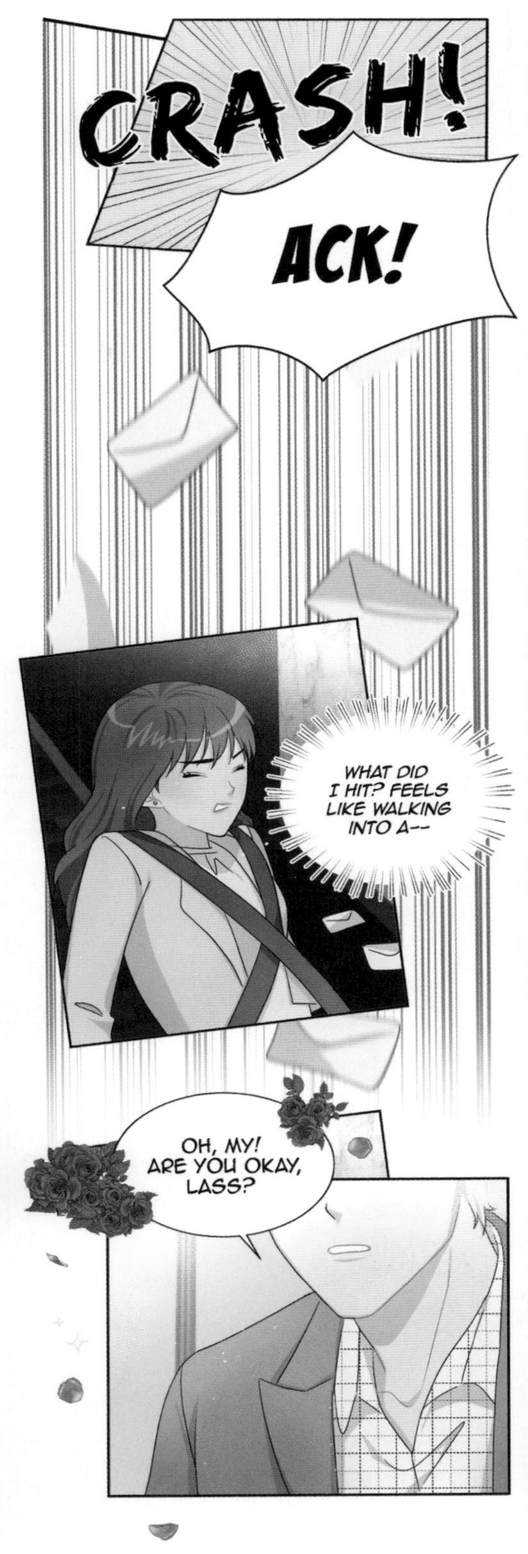
CRASH!
ACK!
WHAT DID I HIT? FEELS LIKE WALKING INTO A--
OH, MY! ARE YOU OKAY, LASS?

BRICK WALL...
I'M SORRY THAT MY INCREDIBLY TONED PHYSIQUE MADE YOU FALL SO UNGRACEFULLY. I WISH YOU'D LET ME HELP YOU GET UP.

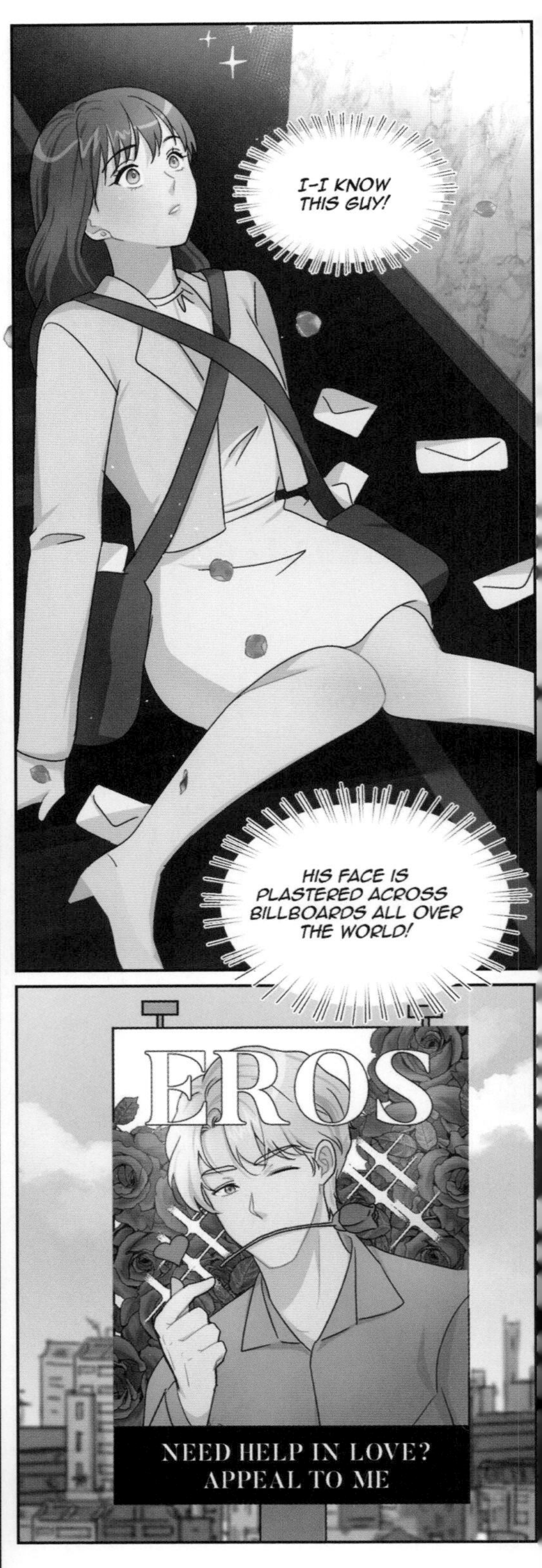
I-I KNOW THIS GUY!
HIS FACE IS PLASTERED ACROSS BILLBOARDS ALL OVER THE WORLD!
EROS
NEED HELP IN LOVE?
APPEAL TO ME

I CAN'T BELIEVE I'M THE CAUSE OF SUCH A PRETTY LADY FALLING ON HER BOTTOM. IT'S UNACCEPTABLE!

HE IS...
THE GOD OF LOVE!!!

EROS IS THE MOST POPULAR GOD FOR HUMANS TO APPEAL TO, ESPECIALLY AMONG YOUNGER PEOPLE.
LIKE ALL GODS, HE WORKS IN MYSTERIOUS WAYS.
waaa
waaa
waaa
BUT PEOPLE WHO HAVE APPEALED AND OFFERED ENOUGH GIFTS TO EROS USUALLY HAVE THEIR WISHES COME TRUE.
Welcome to
Love Wishes
PLEASE, I WANT THAT GUY TO LIKE ME BACK!!! I'LL ONLY EVER APPEAL TO YOU FOR THE REST OF MY LIFE!
I'LL BE LOYAL!
PING!
IT HELPS THAT EROS IS ONE OF THE EASIEST GODS TO REACH...
aww, dear.
I hate cheaters, so don't cheat on me. ok?
Wait for 10 years
100% chance
Wait for 1 year
20% chance

I THOUGHT I DIDN'T WANT EROS' HELP WITH KYO, SO I NEVER APPEALED TO HIM...
BUT SEEING AN ACTUAL GOD IN PERSON IS DIFFERENT!
HE LOOKS A HUNDRED TIMES MORE REGAL THAN IN HIS PHOTOGRAPHS ON THE BILLBOARDS!
OH, A HUMAN? IN OLYMPUS?
YOU MUST BE QUITE EXTRAORDINARY FOR ATHENA TO ACCEPT YOU WORKING HERE! AND SO YOUNG, TOO!
COME ON, DON'T BE SHY! WHAT KIND OF AMAZING CONTRIBUTION HAVE YOU MADE TO THE WORLD? IN SCIENCE? THE ARTS?
WHAT'S YOUR USERNAME ON MY APP?
I CAN ADD YOU TO MY SHORTLIST AND FULFILL YOUR APPEAL AS A WAY FOR ME TO APOLOGIZE...
WAIT...

YOU'VE NEVER APPEALED TO ME BEFORE, HAVE YOU?
I-I'M SORRY...

I CAN SENSE AN UNREQUITED LOVE...HOW SAD.
YOU KNOW, I CAN HELP YOU WITH THAT, IF YOU'D LIKE.

THAT'S VERY KIND OF YOU, SIR EROS, BUT THERE'S REALLY NO NEED TO BOTHER WITH SOMEBODY LIKE ME.
A LOT OF MY FRIENDS AND PEERS REALLY LOOK UP TO YOU AND DEPEND ON YOU. YOU DON'T NEED ME...
Ignored

IT'S REALLY NICE TO MEET YOU, SIR EROS! EXCUSE ME.
SHE'S A HUMAN OF MARRIAGEABLE AGE, AND YET SHE DOESN'T APPEAL TO ME?
what the heck?

CRAP, CRAP, CRAP!
I'VE HUMILIATED MYSELF ENOUGH TODAY. I DON'T WANT TO SHOW HIM HOW FLATTERED I AM JUST BECAUSE HE'S BEING A LITTLE NICE TO ME.
DING!
AH!

HOLD THAT ELEVATOR, PLEASE!
CERTAINLY!
YOU'RE GOING DOWN, TOO?
WHAT IS HE DOING NOW?!
AND WHY DO GODS HAVE TO SMELL SO NICE?!

38
SO... YOU'VE NEVER EVEN DOWNLOADED MY APP.
NO...
YOU'VE NEVER APPEALED TO ME?
NO...
BUT NOW YOU'VE MET ME. DO YOU WANT TO APPEAL TO ME NOW?
I-I WOULDN'T WANT TO TROUBLE YOU...
AH...
...

YOU'RE ONE OF THE WORST LIARS I'VE EVER ENCOUNTERED. JUST TELL ME WHY?
I'LL BE HONEST, BUT PLEASE DON'T PUT A CURSE ON ME...
...SURE.
if I like your answer...
I...ONLY EVER LIKED ONE GUY IN MY WHOLE LIFE.
IT'D MAKE ME REALLY HAPPY IF HE LIKED ME BACK, BUT ONLY IF IT HAPPENS NATURALLY...NOT BECAUSE OF A GOD'S INTERVENTIONS.

I WANT TO TAKE CHARGE OF MY OWN LIFE, AND THAT'S WHY I TRY TO APPEAL AS LITTLE AS POSSIBLE...
YES, I'M JUST A HUMAN, BUT I WANT TO PROVE THAT EVEN I CAN HAVE A FULLY REALIZED LIFE WITHOUT DEPENDING ON BLESSINGS FROM THE DIVINE.
AND RIGHT NOW, I DON'T EVEN WANT TO THINK ABOUT ROMANCE.
I JUST WANT TO DO MY JOB RIGHT AND PROVE TO ATHENA THAT I'M CAPABLE OF TAKING ON MORE RESPONSIBILITY.
DING!
LOBBY
AH!
I'M GETTING OFF HERE. THANK YOU AGAIN FOR THE OFFER!

A HUMAN GIRL WHO REFUSES TO LIKE ME, HUH...

LET'S SEE ABOUT THAT...

ding

WHAAATT??!
Informatio
& Support
I CAN'T GO TO THE FIRST FLOOR? EVEN IF I ASK FOR YOUR HELP?
I THOUGHT YOU WERE HERE TO PROVIDE INFORMATION AND SUPPORT!
I AM CLEARLY GIVING YOU INFORMATION AND SUPPORT--
BY TELLING YOU THAT YOU CAN'T GO TO THE FIRST FLOOR. IT'S HADES' OFFICE AND HE'S NOT HERE RIGHT NOW.
BESIDES, I CAN'T HELP YOU ACCESS THOSE FLOORS EITHER, SINCE I'M ALSO HUMAN.

YOU'RE A HUMAN, TOO? WOW!
WHERE DID YOU WORK BEFORE COMING HERE?
I WAS A VERY POPULAR CHILD ACTRESS,
AND MY PREVIOUS JOB WAS SENIOR MARKETING STAFF IN XX COMPANY THAT WENT BANKRUPT FIVE YEARS AGO...

THAT XX COMPANY WAS SO BIG EVEN THOUGH IT WAS HUMAN-OWNED...
EVEN A SENIOR BECAME A RECEPTIONIST HERE AT OLYMPUS... THE COMPETITION IS CUTTHROAT.
I NEED TO REALLY TAKE MY JOB SERIOUSLY, THEN!
THEN IS IT OKAY FOR ME TO CALL SOMEBODY FROM A LOWER FLOOR TO PICK ME UP?
YOU'LL WHAT NOW, NEW GIRL?

...SHIT.

I FORGOT THAT ANGRY GUY ALSO WORKS HERE... AND HE'S THE VP, TOO.

I'm f*cked

YOU HAVE LETTERS FOR HADES? GIVE THEM TO ME. I'M INTERIM VP WHILE HE'S ON LEAVE.

ACK!
SNATCH!
HEY!

rip
rip
HEY! WHAT ARE YOU DOING?!

THAT WAS A 200-YEAR-OLD LETTER FROM SOME UNKNOWN DEMIGOD. A COMPLETELY USELESS AND IRRELEVANT WASTE OF TIME.
HADES DOESN'T NEED TO READ IT.

THAT... THAT WAS...
THAT LETTER WAS MY RESPONSIBILITY!!!
HOW ANNOYING...

TURNS OUT YOU'RE JUST AS LOUD AND OBNOXIOUS SOBER AS YOU ARE WHEN YOU'RE DRUNK.
I want to know more, but I'm afraid of Dante...
GIVE ME THE REST OF YOUR LETTERS, AND ALSO THE ONES IN THAT OUTDATED MAILROOM.
I CAN SEND ALL OF THOSE LETTERS WITHIN THREE DAYS AND MAKE IT EASIER FOR BOTH OF US.
YOU'RE CONTRACTED UNTIL THE END OF THE YEAR, BUT YOU WON'T NEED TO DO ANY WORK ANYMORE.
THAT'S A SWEET DEAL FOR A HUMAN LIKE YOU, RIGHT?

THAT SMIRK, THE SLIGHT GLINT IN HIS EYES, AND HIS CONDESCENDING TONE...
I CAN TELL THAT IN HIS MIND, HE'S JUST SETTING A TRAP FOR THE NEW RECRUIT,
BUT THIS FEELS MORE LIKE AN INSULT TO ME!!!
NO.
NO?
grip

YOU TORE UP A LETTER THE MOMENT YOU HAD YOUR HAND ON ONE.
ALSO, AS ACCOUNT MANAGER OF INTERDEITIES COMMUNICATIONS, I'D LIKE TO DELIVER ALL THESE LETTERS PERSONALLY.
BECAUSE THAT WAS WHAT ATHENA HIRED ME FOR.

THIS HUMAN...
annoyed
SAYING SUCH AN ARROGANT THING...

YOU KNOW THAT DESPITE THE FANCY TITLE, YOUR JOB BASICALLY TRANSLATES TO MAILROOM GIRL, DON'T YOU?
OF COURSE I KNOW!

STILL...
I'LL GIVE 100-- NO, 110% TO THIS JOB. BECAUSE THAT'S THE LEAST A HUMAN LIKE ME CAN DO.

nod
nod
YESSS! KEEP AT IT, FELLOW OPPRESSED!

...
JEEZ.
COME ON, THEN.
W-WHAT? WHERE?
YOU'RE NOT GONNA KILL ME, RIGHT?
ARE YOU STUPID?
TO THE FIRST FLOOR, OBVIOUSLY. I'M ESCORTING YOU THERE.
He's got a temper, alright.
His only saving grace is how hot he looks.
I agree.
HEY, NEW GIRL!
COMING!
hides

YET ANOTHER
AWKWARD ELEVATOR
RIDE!!!
HONESTLY,
THE HARDEST PART
OF THIS JOB SO FAR HAS
BEEN THE UNAVOIDABLE
ELEVATOR RIDES...

AREN'T
YOU GOING TO
APOLOGIZE?
WHAT
DO YOU MEAN,
"APOLOGIZE"?
LET'S SEE...

FIRST, YOU SLAPPED MY XXXX,
THEN, YOU POURED SUGARY ALCOHOL ON MY SUIT,
STAB
STAB
STAB
NOT ONLY THAT, MY COLLEAGUE HAD TO DRIVE YOU HOME IN A COMPANY CAR, SO I HAD TO FIND ANOTHER RIDE HOME.

K.O.

SO, YEAH. YOU OWE ME A LOT OF APOLOGIES.
ESPECIALLY CONSIDERING WE WORK AT THE SAME COMPANY.
BUT WHAT ABOUT YOU? YOU TORE UP A LETTER I WAS SUPPOSED TO SEND.
YOU INSULTED ME JUST BECAUSE I'M A HUMAN.
YOU DO KNOW THAT YOU HAVE A MEAN FACE AND AN EVEN MEANER CHOICE OF WORDS, RIGHT?
MEAN FACE

IS THIS A HUMAN THING? USUALLY DEMIGODS DON'T TALK BACK TO THEIR SUPERIORS.
I HAVE EVERY RIGHT AND POWER TO DRIVE YOU OUT OF THIS COMPANY.

I'LL TREAT YOU WITH THE RESPECT OF A NEW RECRUIT FOR A VP. THAT'S A GIVEN.
BUT I DON'T KNOW IF I CAN STAY CALM WHEN YOU'RE BEING PREJUDICED TOWARD ME JUST BECAUSE I'M A HUMAN.

HOW ABOUT THAT? PROFESSIONAL TRUCE?

FINE.
DING
opens

NOW STAY CLOSE TO ME.

THE AIR IS CHILLY HERE...
Shivers
AND THERE ARE SO MANY PAINTINGS OF HADES!!!
THE PEOPLE IN THE UNDERWORLD ARE ALL WORSHIPPERS OF HADES. SO YOU'LL SEE A LOT OF HIS FACE WHILE YOU'RE HERE.
GET USED TO IT. I HAVE.

STOMP!
HEY, DANTE!
WHAT IS IT?
HADES STILL HASN'T COME HOME, HUH?
NOT YET. YOU KNOW HOW IT IS.
HA, HOW IRRESPONSIBLE OF HIM TO LEAVE A DEMIGOD IN HIS POSITION FOR SO LONG. IT'S A GOOD THING YOU'RE A HARD WORKER, DANTE.
...
so huge...
so this is the rumored titan?

WHO'S THE HUMAN GIRL?
SHE WORKS HERE. NOT FOR SACRIFICIAL PURPOSES.
sacrificial what?!
ALRIGHT! CAN'T WAIT FOR HIM TO COME BACK, THOUGH.
YOU KNOW IT'S BAD ENOUGH THAT US TITANS HAVE TO LISTEN TO A GOD'S ORDERS, BUT AN UNACKNOWLEDGED DEMIGOD'S?

HA
HA
HA
HA
HA
HA
STOMP
STOMP
STOMP

HEY, ARE YOU GOING TO LET HIM TALK TO YOU THAT WAY? YOU'RE STILL THE VP! YOU CAN REPRIMAND HIM!
JUST INTERIM.

AND HE'S RIGHT. MY FATHER HASN'T ACKNOWLEDGED ME AS HIS SON.
LET'S JUST GO.

JUST PUT HADES' LETTERS THERE. I WON'T TOUCH THEM.

SEEING DANTE'S OFFICE MADE ME UNDERSTAND WHY HE'S ALWAYS ANGRY.

HERE YOU GO.

HE'S GOT THE RESPONSIBILITIES AND WORKLOAD, BUT THE OFFICE DOESN'T BELONG TO HIM. NOR DOES HE GET ANY RESPECT FROM THE PEOPLE HE SUPERVISES...

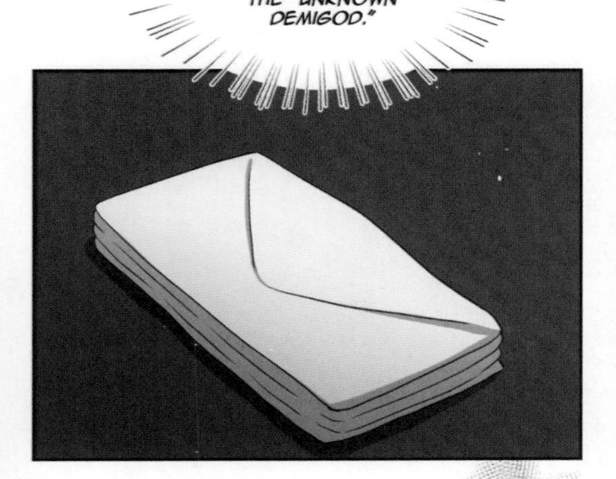
I PUT ALL OF THE LETTERS ON HIS DESK, EXCEPT FOR ONE... ANOTHER LETTER FROM THE "UNKNOWN DEMIGOD."
BECAUSE I HAVE A FEELING THAT DANTE WOULD WANT TO DELIVER THAT TO HIS FATHER, HADES, BY HIMSELF SOMEDAY.

UWAAH...
FIRST DAY AND
THERE'S ALREADY
FAMILY DRAMA...
I NEED TO
SORT THROUGH
THOSE LETTERS
AGAIN.
TA
DA!
huh?
from Eros
WHAT
THE HECK IS
THIS?!
WHAT HAVE
I GOTTEN MYSELF
INTO?!

THIS IS BAD...
I THINK I'VE MADE MY SUPERVISOR REALLY UNHAPPY ON MY FIRST DAY!!!

I DON'T LIKE FLOWERS AND I DON'T LIKE MESSY DESKS.
I DON'T KNOW WHAT YOU DID TO EROS TO SPUR HIM INTO GIVING YOU THIS, BUT THIS IS NOT A GOOD LOOK ON YOUR FIRST DAY.
Some people were here to get a spectacle of you
tap tap

I'M REALLY SORRY...

Sigh
NO. IT'S NOT YOUR FAULT. EROS CAN BE LIKE THAT.
NOW, THE MORE IMPORTANT QUESTION IS...

CAN YOU FIND A WAY TO STORE THIS EXCESSIVELY HUGE BOUQUET?

AH, OKAY! YES, OF COURSE!
I'LL GIVE THIS BACK TO EROS!
THANK YOU. THAT'LL BE VERY HELPFUL.
CAN YOU LIFT IT, THOUGH?
I CAAAAAAAAANNN...
100LB WORTH OF FLOWERS
NO, YOU CANNOT.

750
EVEN MORE AWKWARD ELEVATOR RIDES!!!
The type that doesn't do niceties
BUT DEMIGODS REALLY ARE STRONGER, HUH?

SHIRA LOOKS SO SKINNY BUT SHE'S ABLE TO HOLD THAT WITH NO SWEAT.

I DON'T THINK SHE LIKES ME VERY MUCH, THOUGH...
FOLLOW ME, IRIS.
DING!
AH!

KNOWING EROS,
HE CAN GET A LITTLE
PUSHY SOMETIMES.
I KNOW YOU'RE
NEW, BUT IN THIS CASE,
IT'S OKAY TO PUSH BACK
IF HE GETS TO BE
TOO MUCH...

ADVICE
FROM A
SENIOR!
YES!!!

MY, MY, MY, LOOK WHAT THE TALL BIRDIE BROUGHT ME.

I KNOW THAT MY WELCOME GIFT TO YOU IS A LITTLE EXTRAVAGANT, BUT I'D NEVER HAVE THOUGHT YOU'D BE COMING HERE TO SEE ME!
HOW BOLD!
LITTLE BIRDIE! I REMEMBER YOU SAYING THAT YOU DON'T NEED MY HELP, BUT LOOK WHO'S HERE NOW, GETTING FLUSTERED OVER A FEW FLOWERS!

PROUD
tall birdie...
little birdie?!

FIRST OF ALL, IRIS. YOU SILLY LASS.

I-I'M NOT FLUSTERED BECAUSE OF THE FLOWERS!

IN FACT, I'M HERE TO GIVE THEM BACK BECAUSE THE BOUQUET TOOK UP TOO MUCH SPACE IN OUR OFFICE!

and I'm here because she can't lift it alone.

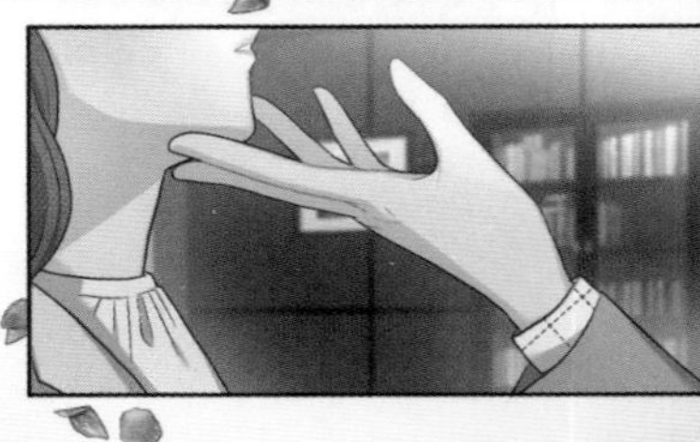

YOU DON'T NEED TO GIVE ME ANYTHING, MR. EROS. I'M HERE TO WORK, AND THIS KIND OF TREATMENT WILL ONLY HINDER MY WORK PERFORMANCE.

NOT TO MENTION HOW IT LOOKS TO OTHER PEOPLE...

What did I do wrong?

YOU JUST NEED TO CALL ME EROS.

EROS!!!

WHAT DID I TELL YOU ABOUT TOUCHING FEMALE EMPLOYEES IN THE OFFICE?!

WHAT? BUT THEY USUALLY LIKE IT WHEN I DO THAT...
don't...

OR ARE YOU JEALOUS?
recovers
X^&@KSD KL?!?DJSK?$#
TRANSLATION: IF YOU WEREN'T A GOD, I WOULD HAVE KILLED YOU 100 TIMES.

EROS, I THINK YOU'RE A GREAT GOD AND YOU'VE MADE SO MANY HUMANS HAPPY WITH YOUR BLESSINGS.
BUT I WILL BE HAPPY WHEN I GET RECOGNITION IN THIS OFFICE.

AND YOU GIVING ME GRAND GESTURES LIKE THAT WILL ONLY SET ME BACK...
DO YOU UNDERSTAND?

YES...

OF COURSE...

YOU THINK I'M A GREAT GOD!!!
AND I HAVE HEARD YOUR CRY FOR HELP AS YOU CLIMB THE LADDERS OF THE WORKPLACE HIERARCHY!
IT'S NOT MY USUAL STYLE, BUT FOR YOU, THE VERY HUMAN DAMSEL IN DISTRESS, I CAN DO IT!!!
uhh...
LET'S JUST GET AWAY FROM HERE, IRIS.

I'M INCREDIBLY CLOSE TO PUNCHING HIM IN THE FACE AND LOSING MY JOB.
HOW DID IT COME TO THIS...?!

SLAM!
flap
flap

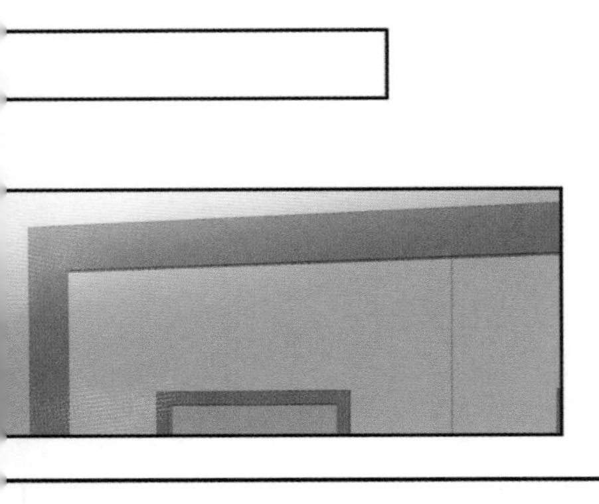

SHIRA STILL LOOKS A BIT ANGRY FROM THAT INCIDENT...

THIS IS MY CHANCE!!!
I'M GONNA MAKE COFFEE IN THE PANTRY, WOULD YOU ALSO WANT SOME?

SUPER BLACK. SUPER HOT. TWO CUPS.
YES!!!

Pantry
THIS I CAN DO...
iced coffee
SHIRA HAS HELPED ME, AND I SHOULD AT LEAST TRY KEEPING HER HAPPY...
AFTER ALL, SHE'S THE REASON I GOT THIS JOB, ANYWAY...
OFFICE IS CRAMPED!

I'LL GET BACK TO MY MAIL GIRL DUTIES AFTER I DELIVER THIS COFFEE...
DO YOU NEED A HAND WITH THAT?
!

AH!!!
GOT IT.

SORRY. DID I SURPRISE YOU?

AH...UHH...
I...YE...NO,
I MEAN...
GAH...
steps away
peeks

I NEED TO STOP STARING AT HIM!
HE'S REALLY HANDSOME, BUT I CAN'T KEEP EMBARRASSING MYSELF IN FRONT OF HIM!
THANK YOU FOR THE HELP.
HERE IS FINE.
tak

O-ORION...
YOU KNOW, THE LAST TIME WE MET...UGH... I WASN'T...
WHERE DO I EVEN BEGIN?
"SORRY FOR PICKING A FIGHT WITH YOUR COLLEAGUE,
AND THEN TRYING TO SEDUCE YOU?!"
I...
I...
I...

THAT NIGHT, I WASN'T THINKING STRAIGHT!!!

...
UM... SURE...

A PAUSE?! AND "UM, SURE?!"
HE MUST NOT BELIEVE A WORD I JUST SAID!!!

W-WAIT! THAT CAME OUT WRONG!
I MEANT, THAT NIGHT WAS JUST--

IRIIISS~~~
OH, HI, EROS.
not again...

I WENT TO YOUR OFFICE IN CASE YOU NEEDED MY HELP.
SHIRA TOLD ME THAT YOU'RE GETTING COFFEE BUT YOU'RE TAKING TOO LONG.
oh, I'm so kind~
DID YOU FORGET WHAT SHE REQUESTED?
IT'S BLACK, HOT, TWO CUPS. DO YOU KNOW HOW TO USE THE COFFEE MACHINE? I CAN SHOW YOU!

HOW HELPLESS DOES HE THINK A HUMAN IS?

I'LL BE TAKING MY LEAVE, THEN.
aahh, wait!

AND ABOUT THAT NIGHT...I UNDERSTAND.

whispers
I THINK IT'S OKAY,
IF YOU'RE A FLIRTY DRUNK.
wha?!

LET ME SHOW YOU HOW THE MACHINE WORKS!
my most favorite human in the world!
tremble
tremble
DOES HE THINK OF ME AS FLIRTY?!!!

SIZZLE
SIZZLE
CONGRATULATIONS ON GETTING INTO OLYMPUS!!!
HOW WAS YOUR FIRST DAY? I CAN'T BELIEVE THAT MY OWN FRIEND IS WORKING AT OLYMPUS!
SIZZLE
SIZZLE

DID THEY GIVE YOU A COOL JOB?
DO YOU HAVE COOL COWORKERS?
I BET ALL THE DEMIGODS WHO WORK THERE ARE BEAUTIFUL.
HAVE YOU MET ALL THE GODS WHO RESIDE THERE?
I...WELL, I'M STILL ADAPTING.
BELIEVE ME, IT'S NOT AS SPECIAL OR COOL AS WE'VE HEARD.
IT'S OLYMPUS, BUT IT'S STILL A COMPANY.

ALSO...DO YOU REMEMBER THE GUYS WE MET DURING OUR DRUNK OUTING LAST WEEK?

OF COURSE I DO! ORION IS SUCH A GENTLEMAN, ISN'T HE?
HE GOT YOU OUT OF A STICKY SITUATION WITH THE ANGRY DEMIGOD,
HE TOOK CARE OF YOU WHEN YOU PASSED OUT, AND HE EVEN HELPED US GET HOME WITH HIS COMPANY CAR.
ah~
WHAT A DREAM GUY...

YEAH... TURNS OUT HE WORKS AT OLYMPUS TOO.
GASP

THE ANGRY GUY WITH THE MEAN FACE ALSO WORKS AT OLYMPUS.
I THINK I'VE RUINED MY CHANCE TO GET IN THEIR GOOD GRACES FROM THE VERY START.
wait...
ESPECIALLY WITH ORION...

W-WAIT! MAYBE THE MEAN GUY WAS A LOST CAUSE FROM THE VERY START, BUT ORION SEEMED VERY REASONABLE AND KIND!
I MEAN, HE TOOK BOTH OF US HOME AND--
WELL, I...
backs off
MAY HAVE...
INVITED HIM TO MY APARTMENT THAT NIGHT,
AND HE REJECTED ME AS COLDLY AS THE BREEZE IN ANTARCTICA.
BOOM
THAT EXPRESSION REALLY DIDN'T HELP, LILY!
ah
ugh, it was embarrassing
AND WHY DID YOU LEAVE ME ALONE WITH HIM, ANYWAY?
YOU KNOW I CAN GET A LITTLE RASH WHEN I'M DRUNK.

well...
FIRST OF ALL, YOU BEGGED ME TO LET YOU BE ALONE WITH HIM, AND I THOUGHT, MAYBE THAT WAS A GOOD THING.
HE SEEMED LIKE A GENTLEMAN, AND YOU JUST WENT THROUGH THAT WHOLE THING WITH KYO AND HIS GIRLFRIEND...
I THOUGHT IT WOULD'VE HELPED YOU MOVE ON...
OH, HE ALSO GAVE ME HIS PHONE NUMBER IN CASE I WANTED TO CHECK ON YOU, SO THERE'S THAT, TOO.

MAYBE YOU CAN TEXT HIM? TO EXPLAIN THE SITUATION AND LET HIM KNOW THAT YOU DON'T USUALLY BEHAVE LIKE THAT?
FOR GOD'S SAKE, YOU HAVEN'T EVEN HAD A SINGLE BOYFRIEND BECAUSE YOU WERE TOO BUSY WITH KYO!
stab
LILY... I FEEL EVEN MORE PATHETIC NOW...

BUT NO, I GUESS...
I JUST WANT TO FOCUS ON MY WORK RIGHT NOW, ROMANCE BE DAMNED.

I SPENT THE MAJORITY OF MY LIFE SITTING BACK AND LETTING THINGS HAPPEN TO ME.
I MEAN, YOU KNOW HOW LONG I LIKED KYO AND I NEVER TOOK THE INITIATIVE.

THEN HE GOT A GIRLFRIEND WHO'S BETTER THAN ME IN EVERY WAY.
THAT'S IT, THEN. I WANT TO THROW MYSELF INTO WORK AND FORGET EVERYTHING ABOUT ROMANCE FOR NOW.

I'M GETTING THE CHANCE OF A LIFETIME I'M WORKING AT OLYMPUS!
I WON'T LET ANYTHING, INCLUDING MY FEELINGS, GET IN THE WAY.
IF YOU SAY SO...BUT JUST TAKE CARE OF YOURSELF.
sigh
THAT GUY SEEMED SO KIND, THOUGH...

Orion

Your friend is asleep. I'm leaving now to go home.

Please tell her to change her locks. Hers aren't very safe for a woman who lives alone.

... typing

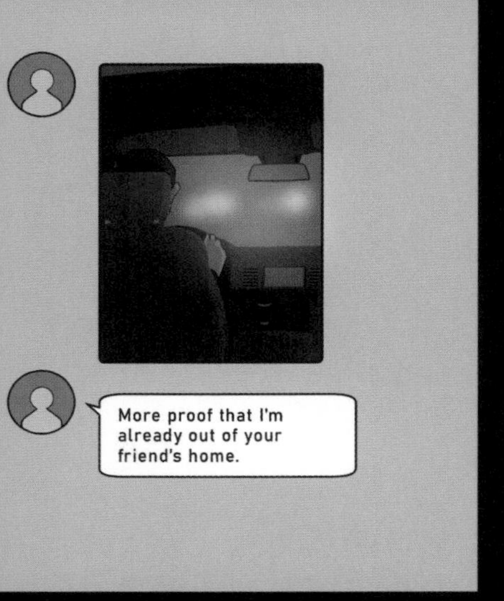

More proof that I'm already out of your friend's home.

THE NEXT DAY
LONG, FLOWY SKIRT,
flutter
A LOOSE, NOT-SEE-THROUGH TURTLENECK,
flutter
LOOKING
WITNESS!!!
SHARP
THIS IS THE ULTIMATE WORK OUTFIT OF SOMEONE WHO DOESN'T LOOK FOR ROMANCE IN THE OFFICE!!!
SHE SEEMS EVEN BUSIER THAN YESTERDAY...
WHOOSH
WHOOSH
(her bags were upgraded to a trolley to carry more letters)

alright we are ready to go
HOW OLD IS THIS LETTER?!
excuse me...
um, can you sign here please?
ugh my neck...

LET'S SEE, WHO'S NEXT...

to: Orion

DAMN! IT'S TOO EMBARRASSING TO SEE HIM AFTER YESTERDAY...

BUT...
Hnnggggg

423
JESSICA, THE RECEPTIONIST, MENTIONED THAT THIS IS ORION'S OFFICE.
what is she doing?

NOPE! NOT MEETING HIM TODAY. NOT GIVING HIM MORE REASONS TO THINK I'M "FLIRTING" WITH HIM!!!
HA!!!
is she okay...?

I MANAGED TO SEND A LITTLE OVER 110 LETTERS BEFORE LUNCH TIME!

I ONLY FLINCHED A LITTLE WHEN A GOD MADE FUN OF MY JOB AND I HAVEN'T ANGERED DANTE OR RUN INTO EROS YET.
WHAT A GREAT DAY!!!
Starting a new batch of deliveries

THERE'S ONLY ONE PROBLEM, THOUGH...

WHAT SHOULD I DO WITH THIS LETTER? IT'S FOR HADES FROM "THAT DEMIGOD..."
DANTE DESTROYED THE OTHER LETTER FROM "DEEDEE" YESTERDAY.
I HAVE MY SUSPICIONS ABOUT WHO "DEEDEE" IS, BUT STILL...
I GUESS I SHOULD JUST HOLD ONTO THIS FOR NOW.
ANYWAY!

TIME TO WORK!
rise
WHY ARE YOU BEING SO ENERGETIC THIS MORNING?

Information & Support
ANOTHER GOD'S SCHEDULE?
SERIOUSLY, IRIS, YOU'VE SENT MORE THAN 100 THIS MORNING ALONE. YOU SHOULD SLOW DOWN A BIT.
you're making the rest of us humans look bad
click
click
I'LL SLOW DOWN AFTER LUNCH.
jeez
FINE, ARES WILL BE ON THE 810TH FLOOR, AND--
ORION?!!!

FOR THE LOVE OF THE GODS, NOT TODAY!!!

DO I EVEN WANT TO KNOW WHAT YOU'RE TRYING TO DO WITH THAT?

JUST...TESTING OUT THIS CLIPBOARD, HAHA!
(bad liar)
SWITCH

IRIS... HE'S GONE ALREADY.
w-wow, what a marvelously ordinary brown desk...

he is?
WHOA, THAT'S GREAT.
Phew
peeks

WHAT'S UP WITH YOU AND ORION?
FREEZE

WELL...
click
WE'RE FINE AND CIVIL WITH EACH OTHER...
BUT I'M JUST NOT COMFORTABLE MEETING HIM...
clack
click
BECAUSE I THINK HIM MEETING ME MIGHT MAKE HIM UNCOMFORTABLE...
clack
IT SEEMS HE HAS QUITE A MISUNDERSTANDING ABOUT ME...
BEING...
A FLIRT...
whoa

YOU? A FLIRT?
BUT YOU LITERALLY JUST GOT HERE. HOW AND WHY WOULD ORION ASSUME THAT ABOUT YOU?
YEAH, NEW GIRL.
PLEASE TELL US THE STORY OF HOW THE GREAT ORION MISJUDGED YOUR CHARACTER.
MUST BE **DELIGHTFUL** GOSSIP.
GASP
(silent scream)

steps away
WHY DO I KEEP BUMPING INTO HIM HERE?!?!
suddenly busy
click
click
click
ALSO...
HE ALREADY KNOWS ORION TOOK ME AND LILY HOME THAT NIGHT!!!
UM, WELL... YOU KNOW, THE THING THAT HAPPENED THAT NIGHT...
I DON'T CARE IF YOU'RE A FLIRT, HAVE WEIRD HOBBIES, OR IF YOU'VE KILLED SOMEONE.
BUT YOU'RE SUPPOSED TO BE DOING YOUR JOB AND YET HERE YOU ARE GOSSIPPING WITH THE RECEPTIONIST.
after that big speech you gave me yesterday
I...
I WAS JUST ASKING FOR DIRECTIONS!
right!?
don't talk to me!

POP!
OH...
MY!!!
POP!
LOOK WHO FINALLY DECIDED TO SLOW DOWN!
LILY!
you again...
IT'S IRIS...
IRIS!!!

I'VE BEEN TRYING TO CATCH YOU TODAY, BUT YOU'VE BEEN A BUSY LITTLE BEE!
HOW MANY OFFICES HAVE YOU VISITED ALREADY?
I DELIVERED MORE THAN 100 LETTERS THIS MORNING.
GASP
more than 100 letters?!

WHAT A GREAT JOB! (FOR A HUMAN)
clap
clap
clap
HERE I THOUGHT YOUR CAPACITY WAS 3 LETTERS A DAY. (SINCE OU KEEP GETTING LOST IN THIS BUILDING)
ARE YOUR FEET OKAY? YOU'RE NOT OVER-EXERTING YOURSELF, ARE YOU? YOU HUMANS CAN BE VERY FRAIL...
applause
eros you dumbass
SEE, DANTE? YOU KEEP GRILLING THIS POOR HUMAN WHEN SHE'S ALREADY PUSHED HERSELF BEYOND HER MORTAL LIMITS!
I HAVEN'T?
100 LETTERS IN A DAY! I BET SHE'S ON THE VERGE OF DYING RIGHT NOW.
I'M NOT!
SHE'S EVEN CRYING RIGHT NOW.
justice
-humans!-
BECAUSE OF YOU!
I MEAN, YOU SHOULD KNOW HOW HARD IT IS TO WORK IN A PLACE WHERE EVERYONE IS NATURALLY STRONGER THAN YOU,
SINCE YOU'RE A DEMI--
ugh will I die if I hit a god? will I be forever single if I hit the god of love?
ENOUGH.

WOW!
A DEMIGOD WHO INTERRUPTS A GOD'S SPEECH! THAT'S BRAVE!
I'M NOT BEING BRAVE! I'M JUST FED UP WITH YOUR CHIT-CHAT!
GO ON, GO ON! THIS IS GREAT PRACTICE FOR YOU!
WHY DOES EVERYONE IN THIS OFFICE HAVE EXTREME PERSONALITIES?
I'm just enjoying the view
my life...

I'M HERE BECAUSE I HAVE A PERSONAL MATTER TO DISCUSS WITH IRIS.
SOMETHING ABOUT HER...JOB PERFORMANCE.
ALREADY? WHAT DID I DO WRONG THIS TIME?

steps

whisper
THE MAIL FOR HADES THAT YOU DELIVERED YESTERDAY...

I THINK IT'S MISSING ONE LETTER...
ONE FROM A DEMIGOD CALLED "DEEDEE."

YOU DON'T HAPPEN TO HAVE IT, DO YOU?

OH, NO. HE KNOWS!

WHAT?
I DON'T KNOW WHAT YOU MEAN BY THAT~
LIAR!
OBVIOUSLY A LIE.
SUSPICIOUS
IT'S FROM AROUND 150 YEARS AGO...
IT HAS AWFUL HANDWRITING.
GLARE
IT'S FROM "DEEDEE."
IT'S SO OBVIOUS THAT YOU WROTE THAT LETTER...
I...DON'T KNOW WHAT YOU'RE TALKING ABOUT.

YOU ABSOLUTELY SURE ABOUT THAT?

WHISPER
oh no, here we go again.
he's going to explode, isn't he?
OH NO...
WHISPER
STARE
STARE
WHISPER
PEOPLE ARE STARING...

GRAB
DANTE!
WHA...
STEP
STEP
WHA...
THERE'S A PRIVATE, WORK-RELATED DOCUMENT THAT I NEED TO SHOW YOU.
COME WITH ME.

D-DOES SHE REALIZE...
THAT SHE'S HOLDING MY HAND IN FRONT OF EVERYONE?

I'M SORRY,
BUT YOU ALMOST
MADE A SCENE.
RELEASE

...

LET'S TALK
ABOUT THE LETTER
SOMEWHERE ELSE.

whoa, she
tamed the beast!
where are
they going?

CLACK

OH, SHE'S BACK.
PEACEFUL~
COOL SENIOR
COOL SENIOR
MAYBE I CAN TAKE HER OUT FOR COFFEE. SHE'S WORKING SO HARD TODAY.

LOUD
ARE YOU TRYING TO KIDNAP ME, NEW GIRL?
LOUD
WE'RE JUST GOING TO MY OFFICE!
CRACK

*DOESN'T PARTICULARLY LIKE PEOPLE. ESPECIALLY LOUD MEN.

Sigh
I WON'T BE ABLE TO CONTINUE WORKING WITH THESE LOUD VOICES.

I'M GOING OUT FOR A COFFEE.
STEP
WHAT DO YOU WANT, IRIS?
STEP
OH?
AN ICED LATTE WITH EXTRA MILK AND LOTS OF SUGAR, PLEASE.
MILK WITH A DASH OF COFFEE. NOTED.

LOUD
HEY, BRING ME A DOUBLE ESPRESSO, TOO!
LOUD

STRAIGHT-TONE
OH NO. MY PHONE RANG. IT'S SUPER IMPORTANT, MY MIND NEEDS TO FOCUS ON THIS.
YOU HAD NO NOTIFICATIONS ON YOUR PHONE!

ANYWAY. YOUR LETTER.

I'M SORRY, BUT I CAN'T GIVE YOU THIS LETTER. IT'S NOTHING PERSONAL, BUT IT'S MY JOB TO DELIVER EVERY LETTER TO ITS RECIPIENT.
AND I DON'T THINK WE'RE ALIGNED IN THAT AREA.
HIDES
AFTER ALL, YOU DID DESTROY ONE LETTER FROM "DEEDEE" BEFORE.

WHAT? IT'S NOT MY LETTER AND HOW DARE YOU INSINUATE THAT I'M "DEEDEE." YOU DON'T EVEN KNOW WHO I AM.
RANT
RANT
REALLY, YOUR TEMPER...
also, learn to be more discreet.
you wanna get fired?!

then why did you even bring me here?

OKAY, FINE.
LISTEN, HUMAN.
I'M GOING TO EXPLAIN THE CIRCUMSTANCES TO YOU.
CHECKS DOOR
LET ME PREFACE THIS BY SAYING I DON'T NEED YOUR PITY.
SO TRY TO FOLLOW ALONG.
DOUBTFUL
who would pity someone like you?

ALL THE EXECUTIVE POSITIONS IN OLYMPUS HAVE ALWAYS BEEN HELD BY GODS.

THERE HAS NEVER BEEN A DEMIGOD VP BEFORE.

I CAN'T SLIP UP. ANY MISTAKE IS GOING TO BE SEEN AS A SIGN THAT I'M UNFIT FOR THIS POSITION.

AND THE ONE PERSON I NEED TO IMPRESS MORE THAN ANYONE IS *HIM*.
MY FATHER, HADES.

BUT...
HE WASN'T... WELL, HE DIDN'T RAISE ME, AND MY HUMAN MOTHER WASN'T ABLE TO DO IT ALONE, SO...
ANYWAY, WHEN I WAS YOUNGER, I KEPT SENDING LETTERS TO HADES TO REMIND HIM THAT I EXISTED.
HE RARELY REPLIED TO ME. BUT WHEN HE DID, I GOT SO STUPIDLY HAPPY.
NOW I'M FINALLY HERE, AND I CAN'T AFFORD TO MAKE A FOOL OUT OF MYSELF.
I'M NOT GOING TO REMIND HIM OF WHO I USED TO BE, A PATHETIC CHILD DESPERATE FOR HIS ATTENTION.
DANTE.
I GET IT.
I'M A HUMAN IN A PLACE FULL OF DEMIGODS. YOU WANT ME TO "TRY TO FOLLOW ALONG?"
I'VE BEEN DOING THAT SINCE THE DAY I WAS BORN.
AH, WELL...
UNLIKE YOU, THOUGH, I HAVE ZERO POWER OVER ANYONE AND I CAN'T JUST START YELLING TO GET WHAT I WANT.

BUT I GUESS YOU UNDERSTAND THAT, TOO, RIGHT?
I...

UGH, I FEEL LIKE THIS IS GOING TO COME BACK AND BITE ME ONE DAY...
BUT...
SHOVE

YOU CAN DESTROY THE LETTER IF YOU WANT.
I'LL TURN A BLIND EYE.
THANKS.

I KNEW YOU TWO WOULD BE IN HERE!!!
SLAM

OH NONONO, DANTE. DON'T YOU BULLY THE NEWCOMER, NO MATTER HOW WEAK SHE SEEMS!
BECAUSE SHE HAS ME, HER PROTECTOR AND NOT-SO-SECRET VIGILANTE!
WINK~

I CAN TELL THAT OUR PRECIOUS VP IS GIVING THE NEW GIRL A LOT OF TROUBLE,
SO ALLOW ME THE LIBERTY OF *PERSONALLY* DELIVERING THIS LETTER TO HADES.
what?
gone?!
IT'S OKAY, NO NEED TO THANK ME! I'M PERSONAL FRIENDS WITH HADES.
I WILL PERSONALLY MAKE SURE THAT NO ONE WILL BE ABLE TO RIP THIS LETTER TO PIECES, ESPECIALLY NOT DANTE.
THAT'S WHAT YOU WERE HOPING FOR ME TO DO, RIGHT, IRIS? SAVE YOU FROM THE BIG BAD DANTE.

DEEP
INHALE
IRIS...

I KNOW, I KNOW! HOW CAN YOU EVER REPAY ME FOR MY HELP, RIGHT?
WELL, YOU CAN START BY GOING TO LUNCH WITH ME~

EROS...

TWITCH

APOLOGIES IF I WASN'T CLEAR BEFORE,

BUT, AS I'VE STATED OVER AND OVER AND OVER AGAIN, I HAVE NO NEED FOR YOUR GIFTS NOR YOUR HELP.

I MAY HAVE GIVEN YOU THE WRONG IMPRESSION AT FIRST, BUT I'M QUITE CAPABLE OF MAKING MY OWN DECISIONS, WITH OR WITHOUT YOUR HELP.
SO WITH ALL DUE RESPECT,
I HOPE THIS GRAVE MISUNDERSTANDING HAS BEEN CLEARED FOR NOW AND FOR THE FUTURE.
TWITCH
TWITCH
OKAY, SIR?
backs away

WHAT EROS HEARD
YOU ARE A HORRIBLE NUISANCE (YOU'RE ALSO UGLY),
AND I'LL NEVER WANT YOUR HELP.
EVEN IF YOU'RE THE LAST GOD ON EARTH! (AND I'D RATHER DIE.)
SOMEONE WHO HAS NEVER BEEN REJECTED BEFORE
AH...
AH...

P.S. Eros will remember this

EROS CRIED...?

HE GOT YELLED AT...?

BY A HUMAN GIRL?!
CRACK

NEWS IN OLYMPUS TRAVELS INCREDIBLY FAST.

DID YOU HEAR THAT THE NEW HUMAN GIRL MADE EROS CRY?
THE NEW HUMAN GIRL BULLIED EROS UNTIL HE CRIED?!
CAN YOU BELIEVE IT?!
EROS CRYING?! NO WAY!
SHH!!!

CLACK
SHH!!! NEVER SAY ANYTHING BAD ABOUT EROS!
CLACK
OH, I ALMOST FORGOT HE HAS HIS OWN PROTECTOR.
YEAH, YOU'LL BE UGLY FOREVER.
CLACK
AFTER ALL, IT'S STUPID FOR
WOMAN TO PISS O
THE GODDESS OF BEAUTY.
CLACK
THUMP!
HEY!

WHERE'S THE OFFICE OF THE GIRL WHO MADE EROS CRY?

IT'S NOT EVEN LUNCH TIME YET, AND I'M ALREADY SO TIRED...
I SENT A LOT OF LETTERS YESTERDAY,
AND I THINK I REACHED A NEW UNDERSTANDING WITH DANTE...
BUT SOMEHOW, I ALSO MANAGED TO MAKE A GOD CRY...
Haaah...

THERE'S STILL ABOUT AN HOUR BEFORE LUNCH TIME.
Sigh...

423

ORION'S OFFICE...
ORION'S OFFICE IS ON THE SAME FLOOR AS YOURS, IRIS!
IT'S ACTUALLY A NEW OFFICE FOR HIM, TOO.
HE RECENTLY MOVED TO THAT FLOOR AFTER SPENDING FOREVER IN THE TOP NO-HUMANS-ALLOWED FLOORS.
DOES THAT MEAN HE GOT DEMOTED RECENTLY?

WHAT AM I DOING SPECULATING ABOUT HIM RIGHT IN FRONT OF HIS OFFICE?
I HAVE OTHER THINGS TO DO.
CREAK

THERE'S A VERY PRETTY LADY STANDING IN FRONT OF MY OFFICE!
ISN'T THAT...

GODDESS APHRODITE?!

Why is she here, though?
REACH

GRAB
SORRY, IRIS.
MMMF!!!

423

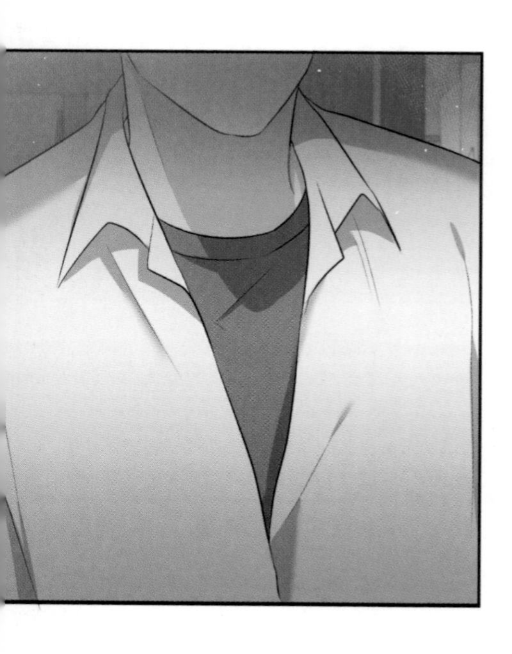

SHH, DON'T LET HER HEAR YOU.

wha... wha??!

SWISH!
AH, I'M SORRY!
I'M...I'M SORRY. I HAD TO SNEAK UP ON YOU SO THAT YOU WOULDN'T MAKE ANY NOISE.
THUMP
THUMP
THUMP

I KNOW THAT WASN'T THE MOST IDEAL WAY TO GET YOU INTO MY OFFICE...
That scared the shit out of me!
I thought I was going to be kidnapped or something!
IN MY OWN OFFICE! ON MY THIRD DAY!!!
YOU BET!
SOB
SOB
IT'S JUST... APHRODITE IS WAITING FOR YOU...
AND I THINK IT'D BE WISE FOR YOU TO AVOID HER WHILE SHE'S ENRAGED.

THE GODDESS OF BEAUTY IS...ENRAGED? TOWARD ME?
BUT WHY?
Am I so ugly I offended her?

YOU MADE SOMEBODY IMPORTANT TO HER CRY...
EROS?!

BUT DON'T WORRY...
SHE MAY BE SHORT-TEMPERED, BUT YOU CAN TALK TO HER SAFELY AND EXPLAIN ONCE SHE'S CALMED DOWN.

MY THIRD DAY AND I'VE ALREADY MADE AN ENEMY!
A goddess, even.
Safely?
Hmm...
She seems worried...

OH.
YOU DELIVERED A LETTER TO ME, RIGHT?
WHY DIDN'T YOU COME IN AND HAND IT TO ME?
I THOUGHT YOU USUALLY DELIVER LETTERS FACE-TO-FACE.

AH...
YOU CALLED ME FLIRTY, REMEMBER?
THE INCIDENT FROM THAT NIGHT STILL BURNS IN THE BACK OF MY MIND!
I JUST CAN'T DEAL WITH MORE HUMILIATION.
THAT'S...

WHOA...
I-IS THAT ARTEMIS? ARE YOU PAINTING ARTEMIS?
OH! SORRY, I FORGOT TO COVER IT BECAUSE I DIDN'T EXPECT TO BE DRAGGING YOU INTO MY STUDIO.

TAP
TAP
I DON'T USUALLY SHOW MY WORKS IN PROGRESS...
RUSTLE

WELL, IT'S NOT FINISHED YET, BUT...
I CAN ALREADY SEE THE LIFE IN THE PAINTING.

HER GAZE IS FULL OF DETERMINATION AND STRENGTH.
HER BODY LANGUAGE SHOWS HER CONFIDENCE IN HERSELF.
THE BASE COLORS YOU CHOSE REPRESENT ALL THE GOOD THINGS SHE'S KNOWN FOR, IN MY OPINION.

I...I DIDN'T KNOW THAT THIS IS THE KIND OF WORK THAT YOU DO, ORION.
IT LOOKS AMAZING.

Throb
THANK YOU.

ARTEMIS IS MY FAVORITE GODDESS. SHE'S THE ONLY ONE I'VE EVER APPEALED TO.
HER STORIES ARE ALL SO HEROIC AND COOL, IT'S LIKE HER GENDER DOESN'T MATTER AT ALL.
SHE'S STILL SO BADASS.
YOU REALLY SEEM TO ADMIRE HER.
AND ALSO...
THIS IS THE FIRST TIME YOU'VE SPOKEN TO ME NORMALLY.
I HAD A FEELING YOU WERE TRYING TO AVOID ME...
I MEAN, YOU COVERED YOUR FACE WHEN I PASSED BY IN THE LOBBY.
AND YOU SLIPPED MY LETTER UNDER THE DOOR, WHEN ALL THE OTHER GODS AND DEMIGODS GOT THEIR LETTERS FACE-TO-FACE.
PSSSh!

I...I THOUGHT...
YOU DIDN'T LIKE ME...AS A PERSON...BECAUSE... YOU KNOW...
I TRIED TO SEDUCE YOU THE DAY I MET YOU!!!
TUG
BUT...
Orion
Your friend is asleep. I'm leaving now to go home.
THANK YOU, ORION...
FOR GETTING ME HOME SAFELY THAT NIGHT...
AND...
FOR SAYING "NO."

...

OF COURSE.
I WAS IMPRESSED. I'D NEVER SEEN A HUMAN STAND UP TO DANTE LIKE THAT.
wha...
AH, YEAH, HAHA...

HMM...
APHRODITE IS GONE, AND NOW IT'S LUNCH TIME.
WOULD YOU LIKE TO HAVE LUNCH WITH ME?

LUNCH WITH ME...
WOULD YOU LIKE TO HAVE LUNCH WITH ME?
HE ASKED TO HAVE LUNCH WITH ME!!!
IS THIS SOMETHING HE USUALLY DOES? OR IS IT JUST A PITY LUNCH?
MAYBE IT'S BECAUSE OF HIS CASUAL CLOTHES, BUT I KINDA GOT WAYYY TOO CHATTY BACK THERE!
HEY, IRIS! GOOD THING YOU'RE LATE.

I FELT A MALICIOUS AURA FROM OUTSIDE OUR OFFICE FOR QUITE A WHILE...
what did you do?
HEY SHIRA,
THAT WAS APRHODITE...
I MADE EROS CRY...

I DON'T GET IT.
I THOUGHT I EXPLAINED WHY I DIDN'T NEED HIS HELP AS PROFESSIONALLY AS I COULD...
BUT SOMEHOW HE TOOK IT THE WRONG WAY AND CRIED.
WOW, IRIS, THAT'S...
YOU'RE... SHINING REALLY BRIGHTLY RIGHT NOW.
What a sight!

SO YOU KNEW SHE WAS THERE AND HID UNTIL SHE LEFT? THAT'S QUITE SMART.
EVERYBODY KNOWS NOT TO FACE HER WHEN SHE'S ANGRY.
IT'S ALL THANKS TO ORION...
HE PULLED ME INTO HIS OFFICE RIGHT BEFORE SHE COULD SEE ME COMING.
AH...
DID YOU KNOW THAT ORION'S OFFICE IS REALLY CLOSE TO OURS?
OF COURSE I DID.
I NEVER KNEW HE WAS SUCH A GREAT PAINTER.
HE'S FAMOUS. BUT YOU ARE QUITE IGNORANT TO THE WORLD OF THE GODS, IT SEEMS.

HIS PAINTINGS ROSE TO PROMINENCE A COUPLE YEARS AGO.

THEY SAY THAT HIS BRUSHSTROKES LITERALLY BRING THE GODS TO LIFE ON CANVAS.

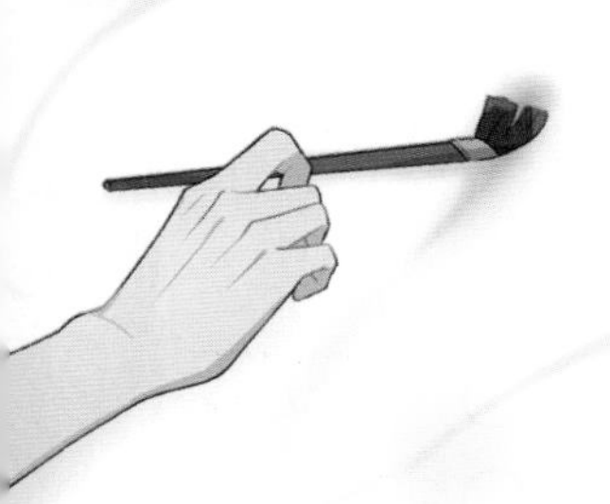

ACTUALLY, HERMES JUST ESTABLISHED A NEW SECTION IN HIS MAGAZINE THAT'S SOLELY DEDICATED TO ORION'S PAINTINGS.

WHOA, SO TALENTED... SO HE'S KIND OF NEW HERE, TOO? LIKE ME?

MAYBE THAT'S WHY HE ASKED ME TO GO TO LUNCH WITH HIM...

REALLY? HE DID? HE NEVER GOES TO LUNCH IN THE CAFETERIA. ESPECIALLY WITH COLLEAGUES.
R-REALLY?
ANYWAY... WOULD YOU ACCOMPANY ME TO LUNCH, SHIRA?
IF WHAT YOU SAY IS TRUE, THAT ORION RARELY EATS IN THE CAFETERIA, THEN I DON'T WANT TO ATTRACT EXTRA ATTENTION.

I THINK IT'S GREAT THAT HE'S COMFORTABLE ENOUGH TO ASK YOU TO A SOCIAL SETTING THAT REQUIRES SITTING AND TALKING, THOUGH.
HE DOESN'T HAVE ENOUGH PEOPLE TO TALK TO.

SO...
GET OUT OF HERE BECAUSE LUNCHTIME IS THE ONLY TIME I CAN BE ALONE.
Also-here's your lunch.
SLAM!

Cafeteria

TURN
ORION'S NOT HERE YET.

MAYBE HE FORGOT?
THAT'S OKAY, THOUGH...THAT JUST SAVES ME THE INEVITABLE AWKWARDNESS OF EATING WITH HIM.

ALTHOUGH... IT'D BE NICE TO HAVE SOME COMPANY.
SHIRA DOESN'T LIKE CROWDED SPACES, AND I DON'T KNOW ANYONE ELSE TO INVITE TO LUNCH.
EVERYONE ELSE SEEMS TO HAVE THEIR OWN GROUPS ALREADY...

MIND IF I JOIN?
THUD

DANTE?
PLOP

WHAT IS HE DOING HERE?!
MILK

LISTEN, SO I WAS ABOUT TO TALK TO YOU IN YOUR OFFICE...
BUT BEFORE I GOT TO YOU, ORION SNATCHED YOU INTO HIS OFFICE.
THAT'S PRETTY WEIRD, ISN'T IT? HE'S KIND OF ANTISOCIAL, SO WHY WOULD HE SOCIALIZE WITH YOU? HUH?
DON'T TELL ME...

IF YOU GUYS ARE DATING, I HAVE THE RIGHT TO KNOW AS THE VP. COMPANY POLICY.
AFTER ALL, YOU TWO DID GO HOME TOGETHER THAT N--
HAHA!
YOU WANNA TRY MY HOMEMADE FOOD? HERE YOU GO!

H-MMFFH-- STOP STUFFING MY FACE WIFF FOOD!!!
DON'T TALK ABOUT THAT NIGHT HERE!!!

ALSO, IF YOU MUST KNOW, NOTHING HAPPENED BETWEEN ME AND HIM.
AND WHAT HAPPENED EARLIER WAS JUST SOMETHING ABOUT HIS LETTERS.

IF YOU SAY SO...
HE'S NOT A FUN PERSON, AFTER ALL. SO STIFF AND FAKE.
HE WAS ONCE A RESIDENT OF ONE OF THE HIGH-EST FLOORS, AND A CANDIDATE FOR BE-COMING THE FIRST DEMIGOD VP.
BUT HE PITY-HANDED THE POSITION TO ME.
what-a-jerk.
hmmm
IS THAT WHAT YOU WANT TO TALK ABOUT? HOW MUCH YOU DISLIKE ORION?
NO, I'M...
YOU KEEP GETTING INTO TROUBLE! SHEESH!
DO YOU KNOW HOW MUCH I'VE COVERED FOR YOU?
hmph!
SHE WAS EVEN RIGHT THERE IN FRONT OF YOUR OFFICE.
THERE ARE PROBLEMS WITH YOUR SALES.
Really?
I HAD TO MAKE UP A PROBLEM TO LEAD HER AWAY.

HEY, DANTE! JUST THE TWO OF YOU? CAN WE JOIN?

OH, YES PLEASE!
WE'RE TALKING ABOUT SOME PRETTY PRIVATE STUFF, SO NO.
wha?
MY CHANCE FOR FEMALE FRIENDSHIPS!

WHAT ARE YOU GUYS WAITING FOR? FIND ANOTHER TABLE.

SHE'S THE GIRL WHO MADE EROS CRY, ISN'T SHE?
SHE SURE KNOWS HOW TO PICK UP MEN. NOW SHE'S TALKING ABOUT PRIVATE STUFF WITH THE VP.

WOULD IT KILL YOU TO ACT NICE TO THEM?
DON'T GIVE THEM THE WRONG IMPRESSION!
ANYWAY, WHAT I WANTED TO SAY IS...
APHRODITE DOESN'T USUALLY STAY ANGRY. SHE BLOWS UP AND THEN SHE'LL REVERT BACK TO HER USUAL CALM DEMEANOR.
Nooo friends
SO I THINK YOU'RE GOOD NOW.

ORION?
I WANTED TO COME EARLIER, BUT I WAS FINISHING SOMETHING.
THAT'S WHY I WAS LATE TO JOIN YOU, IRIS.

SORRY.

IT'S OKAY.
ALTHOUGH...

stare...
hmph
I FEEL LIKE...
MY LUNCH WON'T BE A BREAK, AFTER ALL.

CHATTER
CHATTER
I JUST WANTED TO HAVE A NICE, NORMAL LUNCH WITH ORION. WAS THAT TOO MUCH TO ASK FOR?

CAN'T THESE TWO AT LEAST SAY HELLO AND GREET EACH OTHER LIKE CIVILIZED COWORKERS?!
FWOOSH
SO...
THE WEATHER'S NICE, HUH...?

IT'S BEEN MUCH WARMER LATELY.
DANTE'S NOT EVEN TRYING!!!
OMG

SO, UH... IT LOOKS LIKE THE FOOD THEY SERVE HERE IS REALLY GOOD. MAYBE I'LL BUY LUNCH TOMORROW.
TELL THAT TO ORION.
HE'S THE ONE WHO NEVER EATS HERE.
OH?
AND ARE YOU FAMILIAR WITH THE MENU HERE?
SHEESH!!!
YOU OPEN YOUR MOUTH AND I GET ANNOYED. I SHOULD JUST GET OUT OF HERE!
...
YES, YES. PLEASE JUST GO AND LET ME HAVE MY 20 MINUTES OF PEACE! YOU GUYS OBVIOUSLY DON'T VIBE WELL WITH EACH OTHER!
AND I NEED TO SHOW ORION THAT I'M MORE THAN THE DRUNK GIRL HE HAD TO DRIVE HOME!
UNFORTUNATELY, I'VE DECIDED TO ACCOMPANY OUR NEW RECRUIT HERE.
HMPH!
WAIT...
AH...

NOOOOO!!!
Don't bring me into this!!!

WHAT A COINCIDENCE,
THAT'S ALSO MY INTENTION.

YOU CAN GO BACK TO YOUR STUDIO AND PAINT PRETTY GODDESSES, ORION.
REST ASSURED, I'VE GOT THIS UNDER CONTROL!

I'D LOVE TO GO BACK TO PAINTING, BUT I'M STILL FINISHING MY LUNCH.
...

I APPRECIATE YOUR KINDNESS, BOTH OF YOU. CAN WE TALK ABOUT--
QUICK, QUICK! THINK OF A TOPIC THAT CAN'T POSSIBLY START A FIGHT!

!!
BUNNIES!
BUNNIES ARE AMAZING, AREN'T THEY?

GREAT MEAT.
THEY CAN REPRESENT A LOT OF UNDER-LYING THEMES IN LITERATURE AND THE VISUAL ARTS.

WHOA! HOW DO YOU MANAGE TO SOUND SO STUCK UP ALL THE TIME?

ALRIGHT. YOU GUYS OBVIOUSLY DON'T ENJOY EACH OTHER'S COMPANY.
AND I ONLY HAVE SO MANY MINUTES LEFT IN MY LUNCH BREAK BEFORE I NEED TO GO WORK TWICE AS HARD SO THAT I CAN KEEP UP WITH YOU DEMIGODS. SO--
CHATTER
CHATTER
I'M REALLY SORRY, BUT I'M GONNA GO SIT SOMEWHERE ELSE AND READ MY WEB NOVEL. PLEASE EXCUSE ME.
CLATTER

LOOK AT THAT!
THEY'RE TOTALLY FIGHTING OVER HER.

NICE JOB MAKING THE NEW RECRUIT FEEL WELCOME.

IT'S ONLY BEEN A FEW DAYS!
HOW DID SHE DO THAT?

?

!!!

COME ON, EROS...
HOW MUCH LONGER ARE YOU GOING TO SULK?
BUT, APHRY...
I STILL CAN'T BELIEVE IT. I TRIED SO HARD TO APPEASE HER.
AND YET--
STILL SHE REFUSES TO LIKE ME. I CAN'T MAKE IT MAKE SENSE!

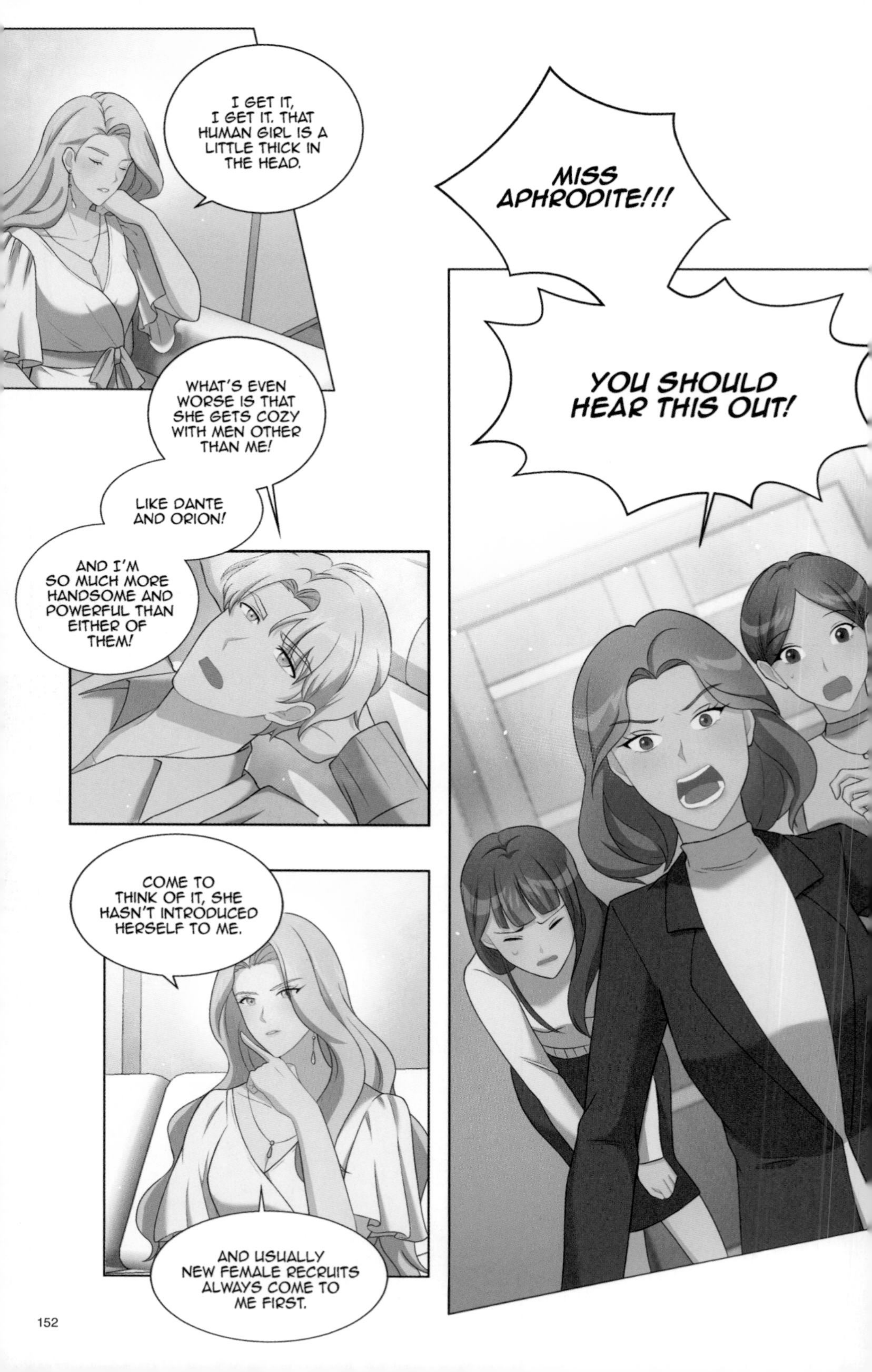
I GET IT, I GET IT. THAT HUMAN GIRL IS A LITTLE THICK IN THE HEAD.
WHAT'S EVEN WORSE IS THAT SHE GETS COZY WITH MEN OTHER THAN ME!
LIKE DANTE AND ORION!
AND I'M SO MUCH MORE HANDSOME AND POWERFUL THAN EITHER OF THEM!
COME TO THINK OF IT, SHE HASN'T INTRODUCED HERSELF TO ME.
AND USUALLY NEW FEMALE RECRUITS ALWAYS COME TO ME FIRST.
MISS APHRODITE!!!
YOU SHOULD HEAR THIS OUT!

Reminder that I'm a god
You're so fast
AH!
HELLO, EROS!
AHH, SO GREAT TO BE ADMIRED BY WOMEN AGAIN.
KYAAAAAAAA!!!

QUICK, WHAT IS IT?
YOU KNOW THE HUMAN GIRL?
SOMEHOW, SHE MANAGED TO GET ORION AND DANTE AT ONE TABLE.

YEAH! TODAY AT THE CAFETERIA!
YEAH! ORION NEVER GOES TO THE CAFETERIA!
AND DANTE NEVER WANTS TO GO NEAR ORION!

I BET SHE'S REALLY GOOD AT PLAYING WITH MEN'S HEARTS.
YEAH! EVEN EROS GAVE HER A BIG BOUQUET JUST ONE DAY AFTER HER ARRIVAL, RIGHT?
MAYBE SHE FAKED FAINTING SO ORION WOULD TAKE CARE OF HER!
AND THAT'S NOT ALL, ACTUALLY...
I FIRST MET HER WHEN A BUNCH OF GUY AND I HAD A DRINK AT THIS BAR...
THEN SHE GOT DRUNK AND WENT HOME WITH ORION THAT NIGHT!!!

IT'S CONFIRMED, THEN...

SHE'S ALSO REALLY GOOD AT ENTRANCING ME! SOMEHOW, SHE KNOWS THAT MY WEAKNESS IS ALOOF GIRLS WHO REFUSE MY HELP!
my pure heart!
for Poppy!
IT'S IRIS!

WE'RE DEALING WITH A VERY EXPERIENCED HEARTBREAKER HERE!
THAT'S WHAT THEY SAID, AND I ALMOST WANTED TO BELIEVE THEM.
clack
clack
BUT I'LL MAKE MY JUDGMENTS WHEN I MEET HER.
IRIS...!

JUST MY LUCK, THEN...
LET'S SEE WHO YOU REALLY ARE...
clack
clack

AS THE GODDESS OF BEAUTY, I'VE MET COUNTLESS WOMEN THROUGHOUT THE AGES.
ALL OF THEM COME TO ME, ASKING FOR THE SAME THING:

POWER.
THEY HIDE THEIR TRUE INTENTIONS BEHIND OTHER WISHES THAT ONLY SEEM HARMLESS.

I WISH TO BE BEAUTIFUL.

I WISH FOR HIM TO LOVE ME MORE.

IN THE END, WHAT THEY TRULY WANT IS POWER.
THEY WANT TO BE BEAUTIFUL, SO THAT IT'S EASIER FOR THEM TO GET AWAY WITH THE THINGS THEY MIGHT DO.
THEY WANT OTHERS TO LOVE THEM MORE SO THAT THEY HAVE THE UPPER HAND IN THEIR RELATIONSHIPS.
IT'S SIMPLE. HUMANS ARE SO SIMPLE. I LIKE THAT.
BECAUSE GODS ARE LIKE THAT, TOO. AND I CAN UNDERSTAND "SIMPLE."

FROM WHAT I'VE HEARD, THIS WOMAN SEEMS TO KNOW HOW TO EXERCISE HER FEMININE GUILE.

THE NAME'S JASON.

William
Louise

AND HE'S ON AN ACCESSIBLE FLOOR...

I WON'T NEED SOMEONE TO ESCORT ME THERE.
HEADING SOMEWHERE DIFFICULT?

?
!

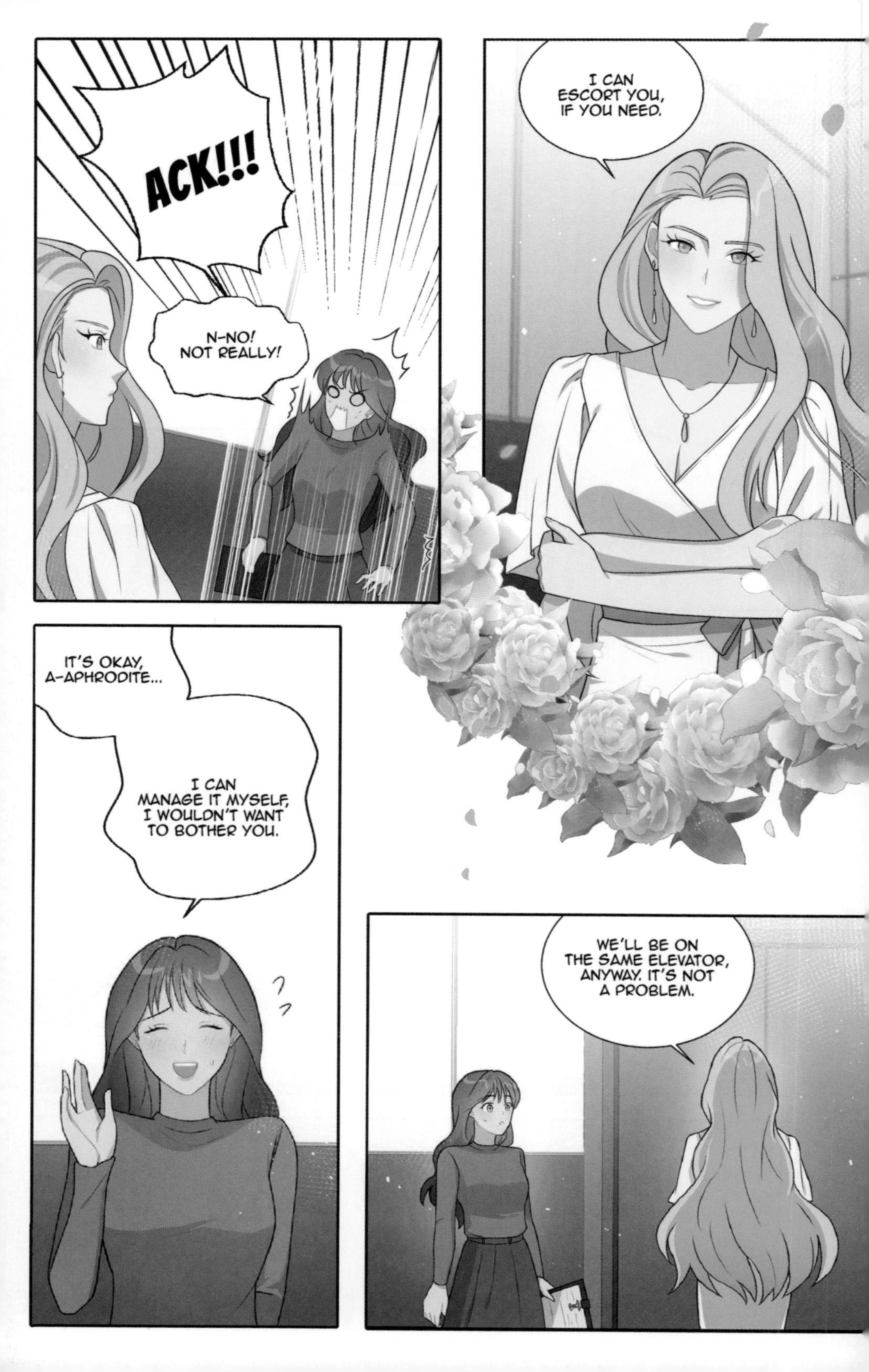
ACK!!!
N-NO! NOT REALLY!
I CAN ESCORT YOU, IF YOU NEED.
IT'S OKAY, A-APHRODITE...
I CAN MANAGE IT MYSELF, I WOULDN'T WANT TO BOTHER YOU.
WE'LL BE ON THE SAME ELEVATOR, ANYWAY. IT'S NOT A PROBLEM.

AH...WELL, IT'S REALLY ALRIGHT.
I'M SURE YOU'RE BUSY WITH MORE IMPORTANT THINGS. I DON'T WANT TO WASTE YOUR TIME ON THIS.

THE STORIES THEY TOLD ME MADE ME IMAGINE HER AS SOME KIND OF FEMME FATALE.
PHRODITE'S IMAGINATION
BUT NOW SHE'S ACTING LIKE A LOST CHILD.

DING

...
UM...
mumble
mumble

MAYBE THEY'RE EXAGGERATING THEIR STORIES?
AFTER ALL, MY DEMIGODDESSES DO LOVE TO GOSSIP.

ABOUT WHAT HAPPENED TO EROS, I SINCERELY DIDN'T MEAN TO HURT HIM.

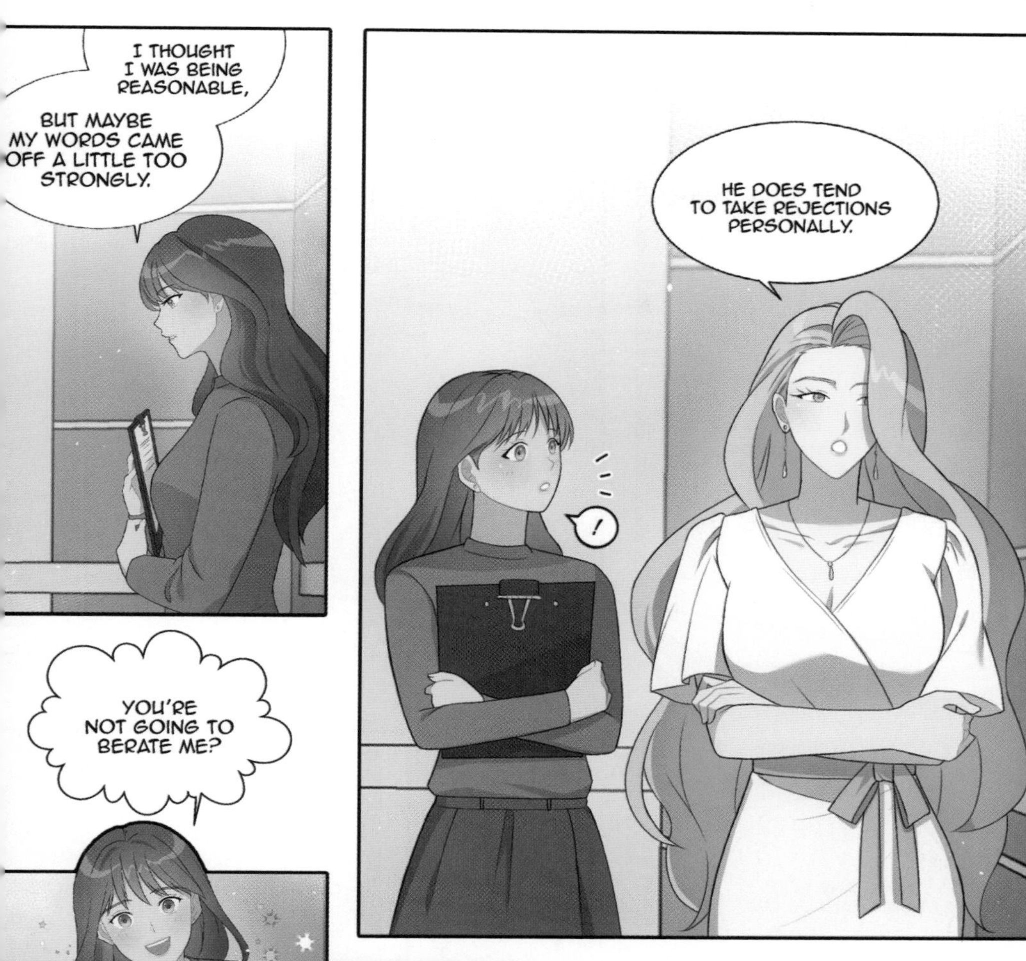
I THOUGHT I WAS BEING REASONABLE,
BUT MAYBE MY WORDS CAME OFF A LITTLE TOO STRONGLY.
HE DOES TEND TO TAKE REJECTIONS PERSONALLY.
!
YOU'RE NOT GOING TO BERATE ME?

I CAN'T BELIEVE I JUST SAID THAT!

DO YOU WANT ME TO?

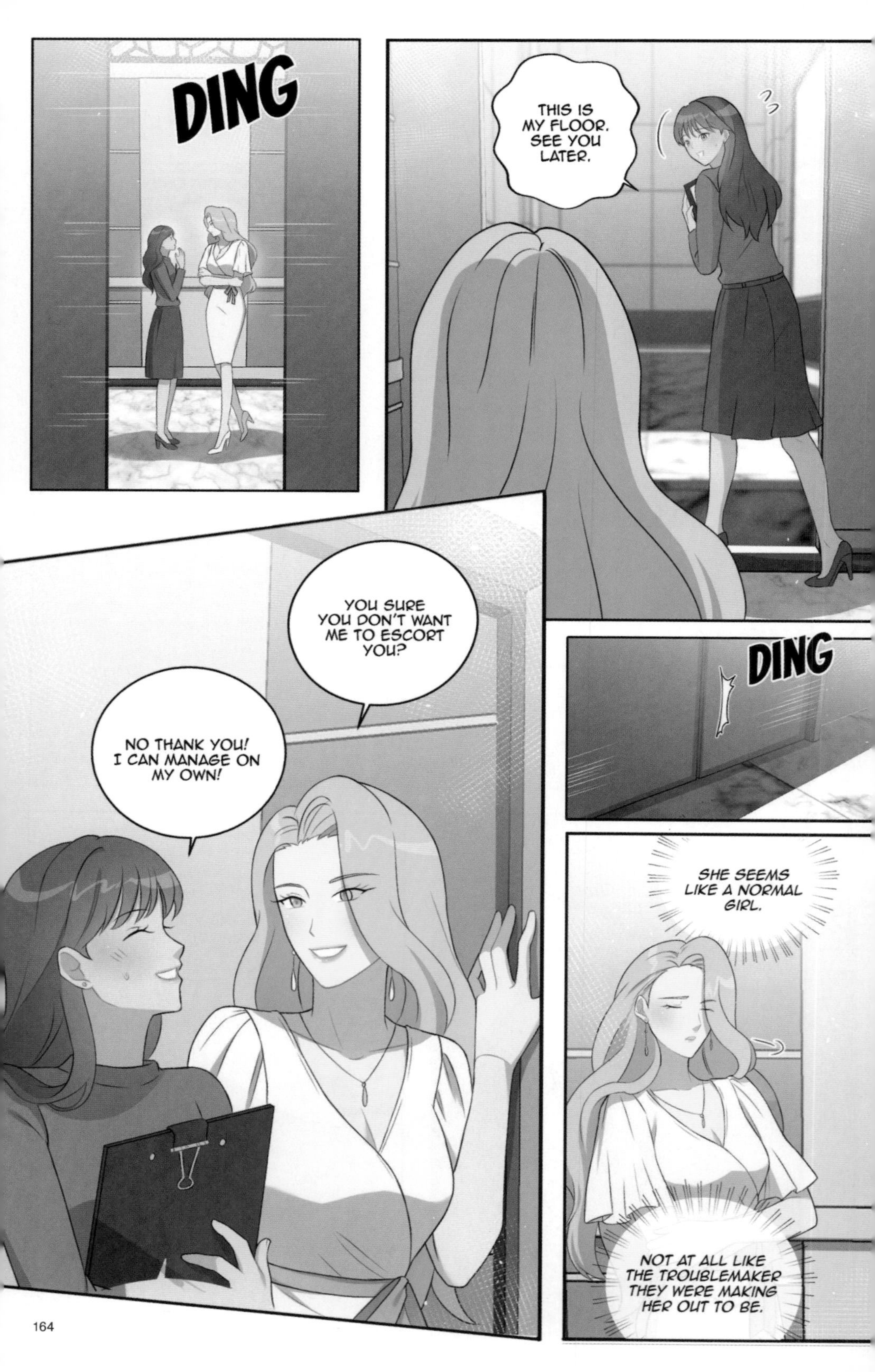
DING
THIS IS MY FLOOR. SEE YOU LATER.
YOU SURE YOU DON'T WANT ME TO ESCORT YOU?
NO THANK YOU! I CAN MANAGE ON MY OWN!
DING
SHE SEEMS LIKE A NORMAL GIRL.
NOT AT ALL LIKE THE TROUBLEMAKER THEY WERE MAKING HER OUT TO BE.

AH! I FORGOT THAT WAS MY FLOOR, TOO!

DING

IS THAT...?

PLEASE, COULD YOU HELP ME GET INTO JASON'S HALL?

I'M A HUMAN, SO I CAN'T GET INSIDE WITHOUT A GOD OR DEMIGOD ESCORT.

THAT LITTLE...

EARLIER...
~INVISIBLE BARRIER~
OH, NO...
UGH, I SHOULD'VE ACCEPTED APHRODITE'S HELP...

!

EXCUSE ME! YOU'RE A DEMIGOD, RIGHT?

THIS GUY'S HANDSY!

AAAHH...

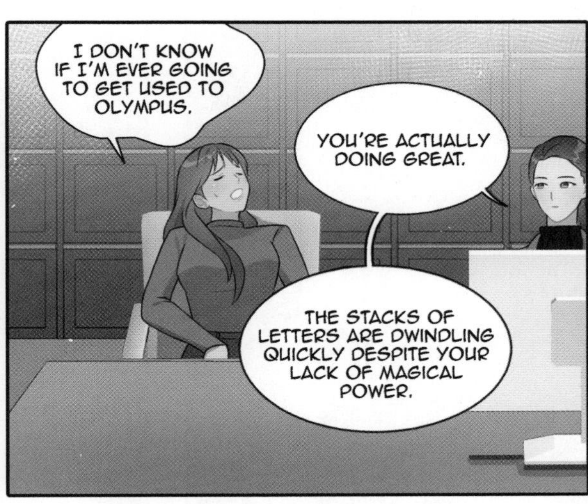
I DON'T KNOW IF I'M EVER GOING TO GET USED TO OLYMPUS.
YOU'RE ACTUALLY DOING GREAT.
THE STACKS OF LETTERS ARE DWINDLING QUICKLY DESPITE YOUR LACK OF MAGICAL POWER.

THANKS.
OH, SPEAKING OF MAGICAL POWERS, THAT REMINDS ME. I FINALLY MET AND SPOKE WITH APHRODITE EARLIER.
SHE'S REALLY REALLY REALLY BEAUTIFUL, ISN'T SHE? I'VE NEVER SEEN ANYONE WHO SHINES AS BRIGHT AS SHE DOES. NOT EVEN EROS!
WAIT, SO SHE DIDN'T SMITE YOU TO DUST?
SHE WAS VERY NICE TO ME. SHE OFFERED HELP, BUT I DECLINED BECAUSE I DIDN'T THINK I'D NEED IT.

THUD!

YOU WERE RIGHT. THAT NEW GIRL IS A SLY FOX.

UNFORTUNATELY, THIS ONE DOESN'T SEEM INTERESTED IN MINGLING WITH US GIRLS.
AND TO THINK SHE ALMOST FOOLED ME.
I SHOULDN'T HAVE GIVEN HER THE BENEFIT OF THE DOUBT.

TODAY IS APHRODITE'S BIRTHDAY.
THE DAY THAT MOST GIRLS WAIT FOR ALL YEAR.

I DON'T USUALLY PARTICIPATE IN GODS' EVENTS, BUT NOW THAT I'M WORKING AT OLYMPUS, I THINK I SHOULD TRY TO BLEND IN.

THE RUMOR IS THAT IF YOU WEAR A FLOWER CROWN TO HONOR HER BIRTHDAY,
YOU HAVE A CHANCE OF BEING THE ONE LUCKY GIRL SHE CHOOSES TO GIVE HER MOST COVETED BLESSING...
...INCOMPARABLE BEAUTY FOR ONE WHOLE YEAR!

I MEAN, NOT THAT I THINK THAT WOULD HAPPEN TO ME.
I'M JUST TRYING TO SHOW SOME COMPANY SPIRIT...

ESPECIALLY SINCE I UNINTENTIONALLY OFFENDED HER BEFORE...

I THOUGHT EVERYONE WOULD B WEARING A FLOWER CROWN...?
INFORMATION & SUPPORT

THUD
NOW YOU LOOK ALMOST INDISTINGUISHABLE FROM THE REST OF 'EM.

I DIDN'T THINK YOU WERE THE TYPE OF GIRL WHO'D BE INTO THOSE SORTS OF RUMORS.
MY COFFEE'S BARELY KICKED IN, DANTE. I CAN'T HANDLE YOUR PESSIMISM THIS EARLY IN THE MORNING.

YOU REALLY WANT THE SO-CALLED "BLESSING OF BEAUTY" FROM APHRODITE?
This place is swarming with bees because of all the damn flowers.

IT'S A MATTER OF RESPECTING APHRODITE.
YOU DON'T NEED A BLESSING FROM APHRODITE, THOUGH.
WHAT?

I-I MEAN, GODS DON'T GRANT ANY FAVORS FOR FREE!
SHE'D DEFINITELY EXPECT SOMETHING IN RETURN, AND THAT'D BE A HASSLE. YOU KNOW THE DRILL.
Also, roses are definitely not your flower.

AH, YEAH, I GUESS THAT'S TRUE.

DING

DANTE, IRIS...

YOU LOOK NICE. ROSES SUIT YOU.
A-AH, THANK YOU!

HE THINKS HE'S SO CHARMING!

OH, MAIL FOR ME?
HERE YOU GO!

WHY ARE THEY LOOKING AT ME LIKE THAT?

GLARE

A-ALRIGHT. I THINK THAT'S ALL, SO I'LL GET GOING NOW.

WAIT.
SLAM

WHY ARE YOU WEARING THIS?

BECAUSE IT'S APHRODITE'S BIRTHDAY!
THAT'S SO SWEET. TRYING TO GET INTO HER FAVOR, AREN'T YOU?

IS THERE SOMETHING WRONG?
IF THIS IS ABOUT EROS...
THUD
STOP PLAYING DUMB!
YOU DON'T HAVE THE RIGHT TO CELEBRATE APHRODITE'S BIRTHDAY! NOT AFTER WHAT YOU DID!

APHRODITE EXTENDED HER HELPING HAND TO YOU YESTERDAY,

BUT YOU WENT AND COZIED UP TO A MALE DEMIGOD INSTEAD!
THAT WAS JUST A MISUNDERSTANDING!

I CAN EXPLAIN! I DIDN'T KNOW-
SNATCH
LOOK, THERE'S BEEN A MISUNDERSTANDING--
SHE WOULDN'T LIKE TO SEE YOU WEARING THIS.

WE'RE JUST TRYING TO BE HELPFUL. I MEAN,
...YOU WOULDN'T WANT TO ANGER APHRODITE TWICE IN A WEEK, WOULD YOU?
YEAH, SHE CAN RUIN YOUR LIFE, YOU KNOW?

LOOK, I DIDN'T KNOW THAT IT WAS THE GOLDEN FLEECE JASON, THAT'S ALL.
IT'S SUCH A COMMON NAME--

YOU CAN GO NOW. BYE-BYE.

OMG YOU'RE SO MEAN!
I JUST TOOK THE CROWN!
DID YOU SEE HOW SHE--
...
CREAK
WHY DO I KEEP GETTING CAUGHT UP IN THESE STUPID MISUNDERSTANDINGS?!

AND MORE IMPORTANTLY, APHRODITE IS STILL ANGRY WITH ME...?

WHO'S BEEN GIVING MY JUNIOR A HARD TIME? IF IT'S EROS AGAIN, I SWEAR I'LL SHOVE HIS **** ***** UP TO HIS ***!!!
WHAT'S GOT YOU DOWN, IRIS?
A FLIRTY DEMIGOD? HARD-TO-REACH FLOORS? PEOPLE GIVING YOU THE WRONG DIRECTIONS? IRRATIONALLY ANGRY GODS? IS EROS GIVING YOU--
NO, NO! IT'S NOT EROS!
APPARENTLY, I MADE APHRODITE ANGRY AGAIN...
YOU KNOW, ONLY SUPER-DEVOTED APHRODITE FOLLOWERS REALLY WEAR THE CROWN AT THE OFFICE...

LET'S TAKE A QUICK WALK.
?

ARE YOU SURE THIS IS OKAY? IF HE'S BUSY, THEN I WOULDN'T WANT TO INTRUDE...
KNOCK
KNOCK

KER-CHACK
HEY!

ORION TOLD ME THAT YOU LIT UP LIKE A CHRISTMAS TREE WHEN YOU SAW THE UNFINISHED VERSION OF THIS, SO I THINK YOU'LL LOVE THE FINISHED ONE.

THERE ARE STILL A FEW DETAILS HERE AND THERE THAT I SHOULD FINISH--
HOW ARE YOU SO TALENTED?

THIS IS AMAZING! YOU REALLY DID HER JUSTICE!

!

THAT GIRL SURE KNOWS HOW TO BOUNCE BACK.

EVEN THOUGH THERE ARE PEOPLE WHO HAVE THE WRONG IMPRESSION OF ME HERE,
MORNING!
THERE ARE MANY OTHERS WHO TREAT ME WELL.
LIKE WHOEVER LEFT ME FLOWERS A FEW DAYS BACK. I WONDER WHO IT COULD'VE BEEN...
I UNDERSTAND WHY APHRODITE DISLIKES ME, THOUGH.
I MEAN, I DID REJECT HER OFFER, BEFORE BEGGING THAT DEMIGOD FOR HELP RIGHT AFTERWARDS.

I SHOULD PROBABLY TRY TO TALK TO HER SO THAT I CAN EXPLAIN THE SITUATION PROPERLY...
CLACK
CLACK

I CAN'T WAIT FOR FRIDAY NIGHT!
ᵘᵘ...
ME NEITHER!
CLACK
CLACK
CLACK

DO YOU KNOW WHAT YOU'RE GOING TO WEAR? I'VE ALREADY CHOSEN MY DRESS!

IT'S THEM!!!

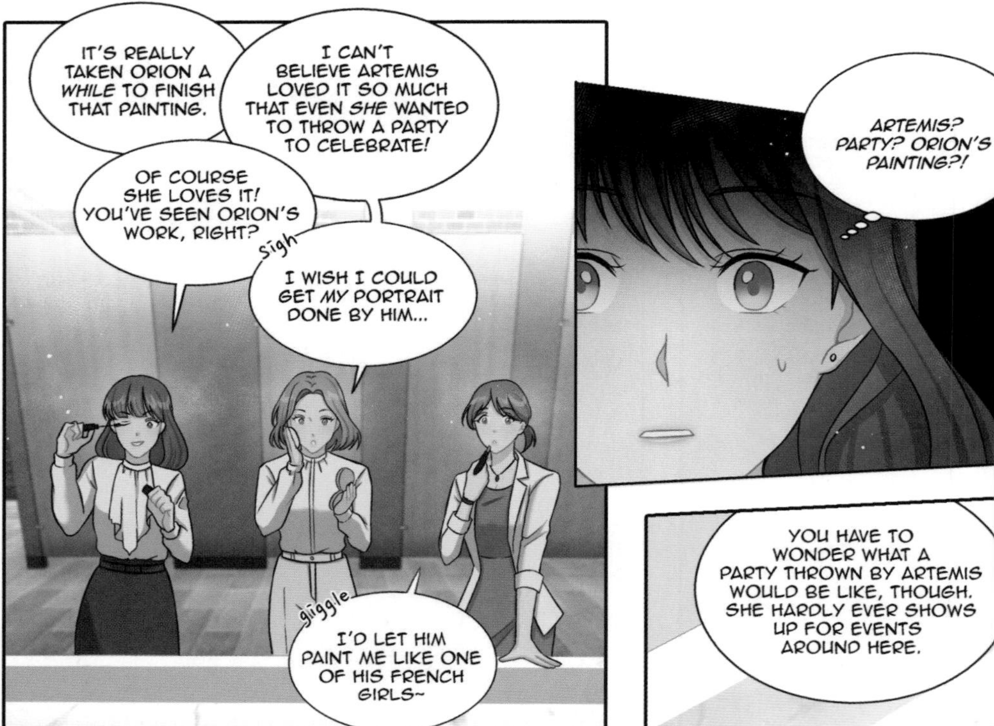
IT'S REALLY TAKEN ORION A *WHILE* TO FINISH THAT PAINTING.
I CAN'T BELIEVE ARTEMIS LOVED IT SO MUCH THAT EVEN *SHE* WANTED TO THROW A PARTY TO CELEBRATE!
OF COURSE SHE LOVES IT! YOU'VE SEEN ORION'S WORK, RIGHT?
Sigh
I WISH I COULD GET MY PORTRAIT DONE BY HIM...
giggle
I'D LET HIM PAINT ME LIKE ONE OF HIS FRENCH GIRLS~
ARTEMIS? PARTY? ORION'S PAINTING?!

YOU HAVE TO WONDER WHAT A PARTY THROWN BY ARTEMIS WOULD BE LIKE, THOUGH. SHE HARDLY EVER SHOWS UP FOR EVENTS AROUND HERE.
YEAH, THAT'S TRUE. SHE'S THE LAST OLYMPIAN TO GET A PAINTING.

LAST *RELEVANT* OLYMPIAN, THAT IS!
HEY, DO YOU THINK THAT THE CUTE HUMAN INTERN IS GONNA COME?
NO WAY! HE'D PROBABLY FEEL SO OUT OF PLACE!
LOL
WELL, HUMANS ARE INVITED! YOU KNOW HOW MUCH ARTEMIS LOVES THEM... SOME SAY SHE LOVES THEM EVEN *MORE* THAN DEMIGODS!
EWWWW~ DON'T TELL ME YOU'RE ACTUALLY CRUSHING ON A HUMAN!

SO I'M... INVITED, TOO?

SLAM!
DID YOU KNOW THAT ARTEMIS IS THROWING A PARTY?!

YES, I HEARD.
EH?
WHAT?! WHY DIDN'T YOU TELL ME?!
I FORGOT.

ALSO, PARTIES AREN'T REALLY MY THING.
mountain of iris' unsent letters
rustle
rustle

HERE YOU GO.
artemis

uwaaa
SNIIIIFF-
IT SMELLS LIKE HEAVEN...
THAT WAS BURIED UNDER MOLDY LETTERS FOR DAYS.
THAT'S BECAUSE YOU DIDN'T TELL ME ABOUT IT!
sniff sniff
GRRR!
IRIS... IT'S UP TO YOU, BUT...
I WOULDN'T RECOMMEND GOING.

WHAT? WHY NOT? I HEARD THAT ALL HUMANS ARE INVITED!

I'M GOING TO ASK JESSICA IF SHE'S GOING, TOO!

SLAM
WELL, LET'S HOPE THAT JESSICA CAN KNOCK SOME SENSE INTO HER.

pew
pew

JESSICA!
Startled

OH, IT'S JUST YOU.
HA. WERE YOU SLACKING OFF?
Sigh

SO, ARE YOU GOING TO ARTEMIS' PARTY?
NO.

I CAN UNDERSTAND IF IT'S SHIRA...
BUT JESSICA, TOO!?

YOU DON'T UNDERSTAND WHAT THIS IS ABOUT, DO YOU?
SOMETIMES OLYMPUS THROWS BIG PARTIES LIKE THIS WHEN ONE OF THE RELEVANT OLYMPIANS WANTS TO CELEBRATE SOME OCCASION OR THE OTHER.

AND IT'S NEVER A GOOD IDEA FOR US HUMANS TO BE THERE.

YOU KNOW THAT THERE'S A CERTAIN GROUP OF... UGH, PEOPLE WHO DON'T LIKE YOU, RIGHT?
ESPECIALLY WHEN...
whisper whisper

GULP
WOW, GOSSIP REALLY DOES GET AROUND HERE.

THAT'S THE THING, THOUGH.

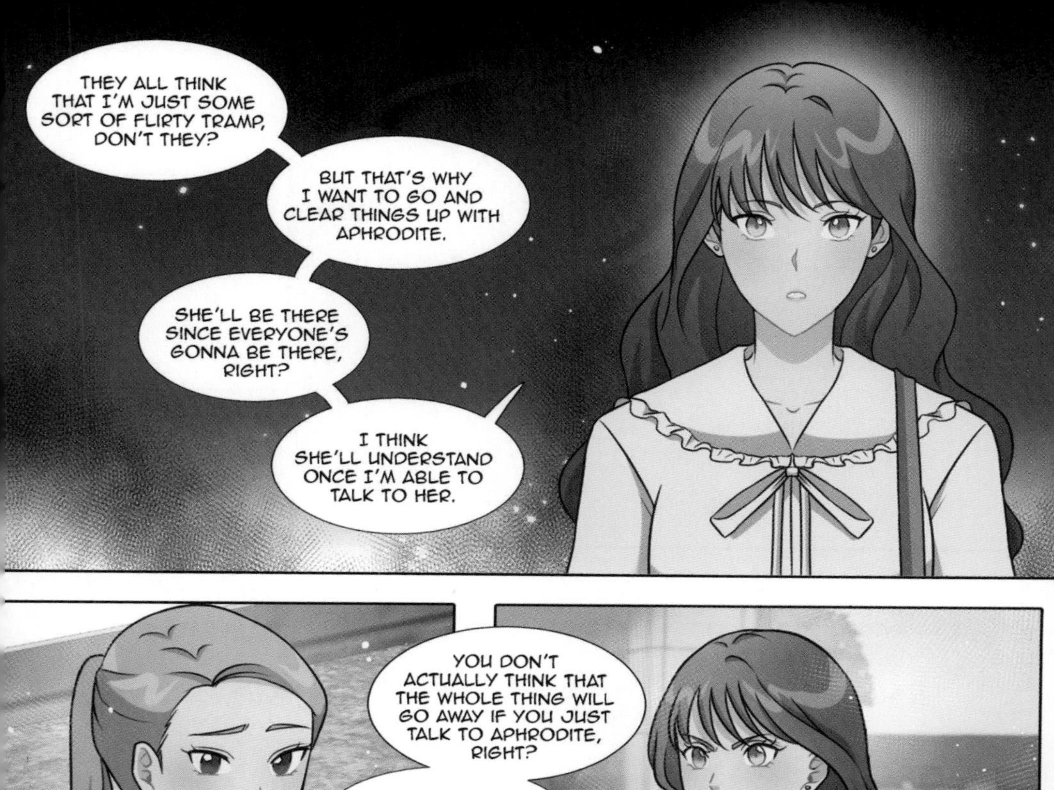
THEY ALL THINK THAT I'M JUST SOME SORT OF FLIRTY TRAMP, DON'T THEY?
BUT THAT'S WHY I WANT TO GO AND CLEAR THINGS UP WITH APHRODITE.
SHE'LL BE THERE SINCE EVERYONE'S GONNA BE THERE, RIGHT?
I THINK SHE'LL UNDERSTAND ONCE I'M ABLE TO TALK TO HER.

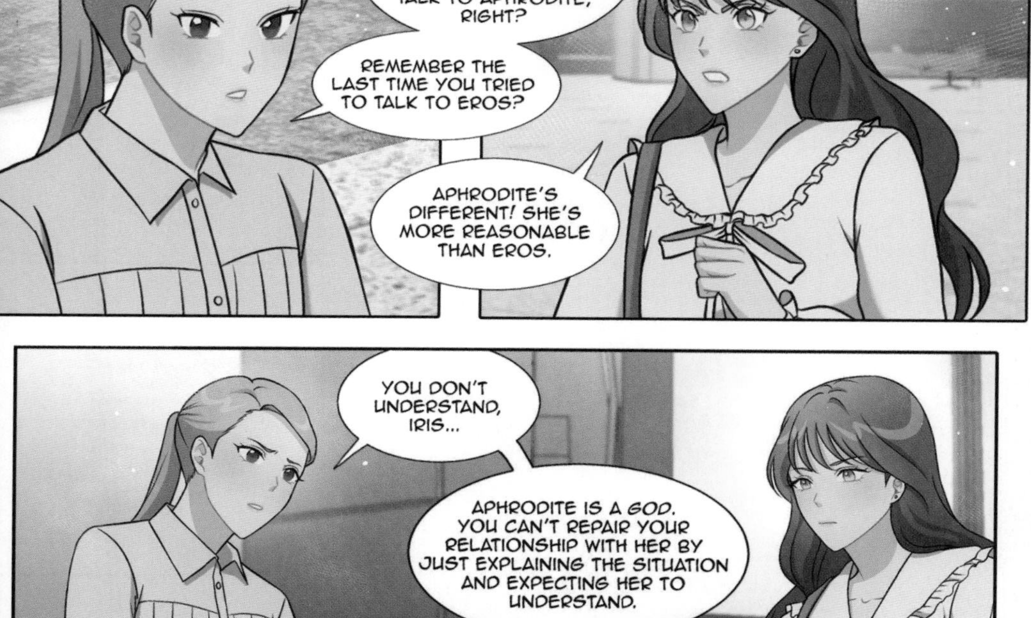
YOU DON'T ACTUALLY THINK THAT THE WHOLE THING WILL GO AWAY IF YOU JUST TALK TO APHRODITE, RIGHT?
REMEMBER THE LAST TIME YOU TRIED TO TALK TO EROS?
APHRODITE'S DIFFERENT! SHE'S MORE REASONABLE THAN EROS.
YOU DON'T UNDERSTAND, IRIS...
APHRODITE IS A *GOD*. YOU CAN'T REPAIR YOUR RELATIONSHIP WITH HER BY JUST EXPLAINING THE SITUATION AND EXPECTING HER TO UNDERSTAND.
WE HUMANS ONLY GET ONE CHANCE WITH THEM, AND IF WE BLOW IT, THEN THEY'LL NEVER BOTHER WITH US AGAIN.

AFTER ALL, THEY'VE LIVED FOR THOUSANDS OF YEARS AND WILL LIVE FOR THOUSANDS MORE. WE'RE ONLY PRESENT FOR A TINY FRACTION OF THEIR LIVES. IT'S NOT WORTH IT FOR THEM TO CARE.
WE JUST... DON'T MATTER THAT MUCH.
I DON'T THINK THAT'S TRUE.
I MEAN, I HAVEN'T BEEN WORKING HERE THAT LONG, AND I KNOW I'VE GOTTEN CAUGHT UP IN A FEW MISUNDERSTANDINGS,
BUT...
I DON'T THINK THAT WE'RE INSIGNIFICANT TO *ALL* THE GODS.
AT LEAST, THAT'S WHAT I STILL CHOOSE TO BELIEVE.
IRIS...
I HOPE THAT YOU'RE RIGHT.

ORION?!
DING

DAMN IT, IRIS. YOU CAN'T TURN INTO JELLY WHENEVER HE SMILES AT YOU!
YOU LIKE LOTS OF SUGAR AND CREAM, RIGHT?
ACTUALLY, I'VE BEEN MEANING TO TALK TO YOU. I HAVE GOOD NEWS.
?
ah, thank you

GOOD NEWS?
I SPOKE TO ARTEMIS WHEN I GAVE THE PAINTING TO HER. I TOLD HER ABOUT YOU.
SHE AGREED TO CHAT WITH YOU FOR FIVE MINUTES, AFTER THE PARTY.

THANK YOU!!!

YOU'RE THE FIRST PERSON TODAY WHO'S ACTUALLY ENCOURAGED ME TO ATTEND THE PARTY.
THAT MEANS A LOT TO ME. AND... YOU ALSO JUST GAVE ME A WONDERFUL GIFT--

--A FIVE MINUTE CONVERSATION WITH ARTEMIS! IT'S GOOD THAT I'LL HAVE FIVE MINUTES,
BECAUSE I MIGHT SPEND THE FIRST FOUR MINUTES HYPERVENTILATING!
A-AH!
S-SORRY! I--
IT'S OKAY. THAT WAS NICE--
UH, I MEAN--
GULP
IN THAT CASE, I'LL BE GOING BACK TO MY STUDIO. I'LL SEE YOU AT THE PARTY, IRIS.

ORION IS ALWAYS SO COOL AND COMPOSED...
THINGS WILL BE FINE IF HE'S THERE, RIGHT?

CLACK
CLACK

CAN YOU LIEVE IT? SHE'S NGING A CHANGE OF CLOTHES!
SHE'S REALLY COMING TO ARTEMIS' EVENT?
DID NOBODY TELL HER?

DING

WAIT!

Pfft-
ROUGH MORNING, DANTE?
huff
huff

ARE YOU OUT OF YOUR MIND? DO YOU REALLY PLAN TO GO TO ARTEMIS' PARTY?
HUFF
HUFF

WOULD IT REALLY BE SO HORRIBLE FOR ME TO GO? EVERYONE IS INVITED.
IT ALSO GOES WITHOUT SAYING THAT HUMANS ARE DISCOURAGED FROM ATTENDING.
OF COURSE YOU'D SAY SOMETHING LIKE THAT.

YOU KNOW THAT'S NOT WHAT I MEANT!
BAM
IT'S JUST...

IT'S JUST...?

BLUSH-

IT'S GENERALLY WELL-KNOWN THAT HUMANS WON'T REALLY ENJOY A PARTY THAT'S CATERED TO GODS AND THE LIKES--
LOOKS AWAY

W-WHAT ARE YOU DOING?
A CHANGE OF CLOTHES...
MY MAKE UP BAG...

WIPES AND A TOOTHBRUSH...
PLACE
...MY FOOD, AND MY OWN DRINKS AND SNACKS FOR THE PARTY.

I KNOW THAT THE GODS' FOOD AND DRINK ARE TOO MUCH FOR HUMANS. I'M NOT STUPID. THAT'S WHY I'M BRINGING MY OWN STUFF.
I WANT TO BE THERE. AND I'VE COME PREPARED.

WHY IS IT SO IMPORTANT FO YOU TO COME?

A FEW REASONS, ACTUALLY.
I WANT TO MEET WITH APHRODITE AND EXPLAIN MYSELF TO HER.
I WANT TO SEE ARTEMIS,

AND MAYBE I'M A MASOCHIST, BUT I'D REALLY LIKE TO SEE WHAT KIND OF PARTY ALL THE OTHER HUMANS IN OLYMPUS AVOID.

YOU--

DING!

SO, I'LL SEE YOU SOON!

DING

WOW, I ACTED ALL CONFIDENTLY THIS MORNING,
BUT I'M STILL NERVOUS AFTER ALL.
YOU'RE REALLY INSISTING ON GOING?
OF COURSE! ARTEMIS WILL BE GIVING ME FIVE MINUTES OF HER UNDIVIDED ATTENTION!
IN THAT CASE...
SPARKLE
FWOOSH
HOW COME IT'S SO EASY FOR YOU TO LOOK SO GOOD?
STOP STARING!

I'M CHANGING, TOO!

SLUMP

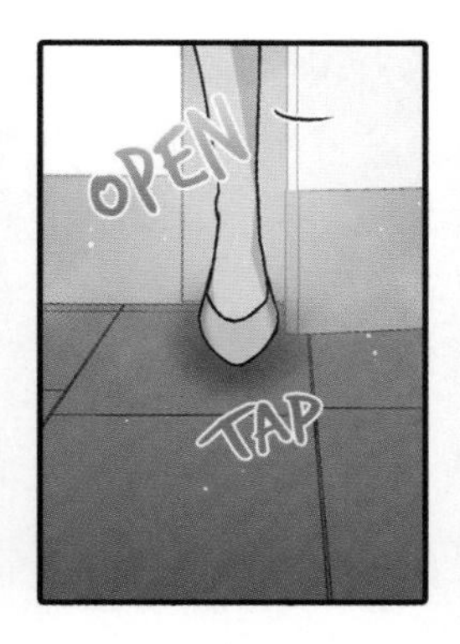
OPEN
TAP

GLANCE
READY TO GO, SHIRA?

SPARKLE

WOW, IT'S BEEN A WHILE SINCE I'VE GOTTEN DRESSED UP LIKE THIS.

YOUR DRESS IS TOO NICE. YOU CAN'T LOOK TOO NICE!

LET'S GET YOU TO YOUR FIRST OLYMPUS OFFICE PARTY.

WHOA! OLYMPIANS SURE ARE SOMETHING ELSE!
chatter
chatter
chatter

WELCOME, WELCOME TO MY HUMBLE ABODE!
WE'RE ALL HERE BECAUSE A TRULY MAGICAL THING HAS OCCURRED: OUR ELUSIVE, VERY OWN ARTEMIS HAS FINALLY AGREED TO HAVE HER BEAUTIFUL VISAGE IMMORTALIZED IN A PORTRAIT!
CLAP
CLAP
CLAP
IN FACT, SHE'S GRACING US WITH HER PRESENCE RIGHT NOW! THIS ONLY HAPPENS ONCE IN A BLUE MOON, QUITE LITERALLY!

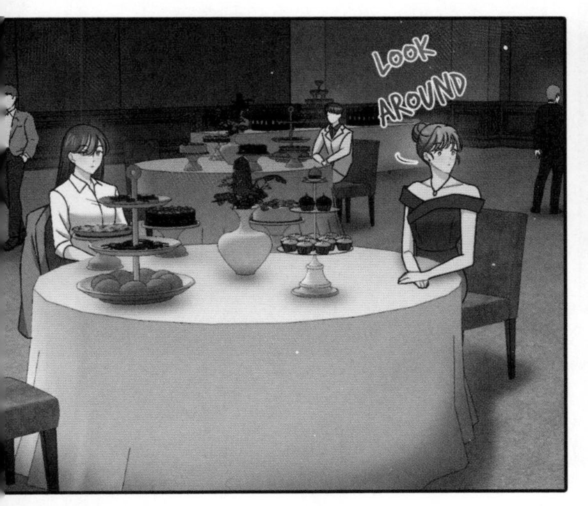
LOOK AROUND

TMP

A NERVOUS EATER

NOD

pat
WAVE
WAVE

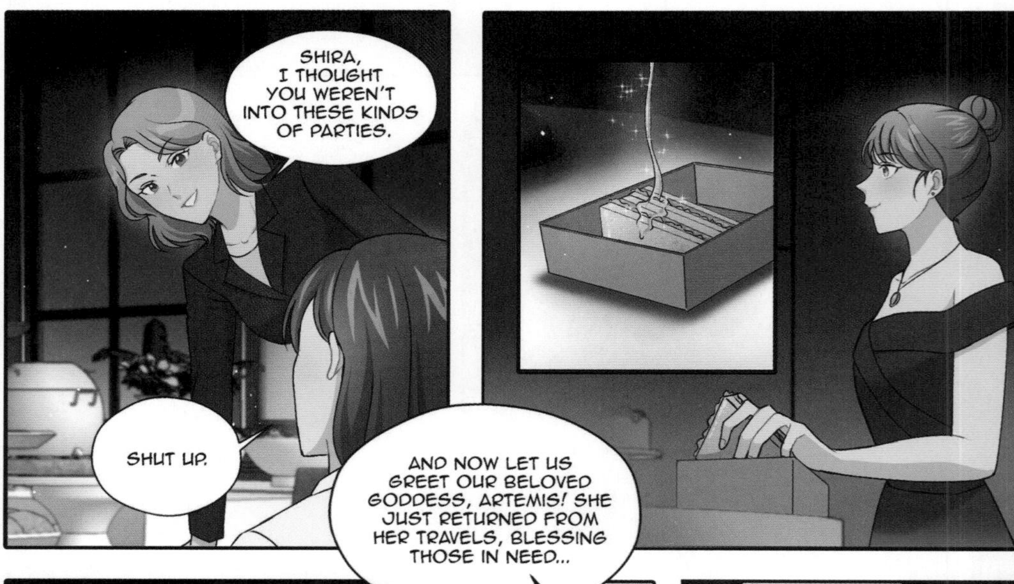
SHIRA, I THOUGHT YOU WEREN'T INTO THESE KINDS OF PARTIES.
SHUT UP.
AND NOW LET US GREET OUR BELOVED GODDESS, ARTEMIS! SHE JUST RETURNED FROM HER TRAVELS, BLESSING THOSE IN NEED...

IF THE HUMAN COMES BUT DOESN'T TRY ANY OF OUR FOOD...
WHAT'S THE POINT, RIGHT?
giggles

OH MY GOD, OH MY GOD, OH MY GOD, SHE'S HERE!
munch

COUGH!
YOU'RE LOOKING A BIT FAINT. DO YOU WANT SOME WATER?
NO, THANK YOU. I BROUGHT...
...MY OWN...
WHOA... WHY DO I FEEL SO...LIGHT?

OH NO, OH NO, OH NO! I MESSED UP!

Huff

Huff

I THOUGHT SHE'D CHASE AFTER ME... BUT I SHOULD HAVE KNOWN BETTER.
FWOOSH
I DON'T EVEN HAVE A PHONE...
AND NOW, I'M LOST...
OR SHOES...
TAP
TAP
Huh?
THERE'S A LIGHT THERE! MAYBE THEY CAN HELP ME!

GLANCE
!
WHAT ARE YOU DOING HERE?
IS SHE...

SHE DOESN'T
LOOK HUMAN! IS
SHE A DEMIGOD?
?
MOM DOESN'T REALLY TELL ME MUCH ABOUT THE GODS, SO I DON'T KNOW IF SHE'S ONE OF THEM...
I'M ARTEMIS.
FWIP
STARTLED
shudder
ARE YOU LOST? YOU LOOK FRIGHTENED.
I-I'M NOT!
I DON'T NEED YOUR HELP. YOU'RE JUST GOING TO DEMAND HALF OF MY LIFE OR SOMETHING!
HM?
THAT'S WHAT MY MOTHER TAUGHT ME. DON'T ASK FOR FAVORS FROM GODS, BECAUSE THEY'LL ASK FOR TEN TIMES MORE THAN YOU CAN GIVE.
YOU'RE A GOD, RIGHT? I CAN TELL BECAUSE YOU LOOK SO BEAUTIFUL.

OH, LITTLE GIRL. IS THAT HOW MY SIBLINGS HAVE TREATED YOU?
DON'T WORRY. I WON'T ASK YOU FOR ANYTHING.
LET ME HELP YOU GET HOME. THEN I'LL BE OUT OF YOUR LIFE.
OH MY GOD, DO YOU SEE HER GETTING CROSS-EYED?
HOW MUCH NECTAR DID YOU GIVE HER?
HEEHEE. HEHE.

IRIS? WHAT'S SO FUNNY?
YOUR HAIR IS FUNNY! HAHAHA. YOU LOOK SO PRETTY THOUGH...

IS THIS HOW YOU GET WHEN YOU'RE NERVOUS? GET IT TOGETHER!

sniff
sniff

WHICH ONE OF YOU SPIKED HER FOOD?
SHE BROUGHT HER OWN FOOD AND DRINKS, AND YOU STILL MESSED WITH HER?!
hehe

THE RELATIONSHIP BETWEEN GODS AND HUMANS HAS ALWAYS BEEN FICKLE. I HOPE THAT MOVING FORWARD, WE CAN BE MORE CONSIDERATE TOWARD HUMANS...

WHOA, ARTEMIS IS REALLY HERE...
IT'S NOTHING DANGEROUS!
WHY, YOU--
BAM

TAP
TAP

...

GLANCE

HEHE
I'VE MISSED YO
MS. ARTEMIS!

WHAT THE--?

IT'S ONLY BEEN TEN YEARS SINCE I RETURNED TO OLYMPUS AND ACCEPTED MY PLACE AS AN OLYMPIAN, BUT I'VE BEEN TRULY TOUCHED BY THE SINCERITY AND DEDICATION OF THIS YOUNG ARTIST.

PLEASE WELCOME ORION!

CLAP
CLAP
CLAP
CLAP

THUD!

CAN YOU HEAR ME? MS. ARTEMIS~ YOU'RE THE ONLY GODDESS I'LL EVER LIKE!
SWAY
SWAY

MURMUR
MURMUR

MURMUR
MURMUR

YES, THANK YOU. PLEASE ALLOW ME TO PRESENT YOUR PORTRAIT...
I HEAR MY NAME BEING CALLED...
MURMUR
MURMUR
MURMUR
EVERYONE'S CALLING YOUR NAME. YOU'RE ONSTAGE...
IS THAT SO...
I'M TRYING MY BEST HERE, BUT I CAN'T AVOID GODS AND DEMIGODS FOREVER.
UNFORTUNATELY, MOST OF THEM AREN'T LIKE YOU, MS. ARTEMIS...

I DON'T WANT TO GIVE UP, THOUGH...
ALTHOUGH IT'D BE NICE IF I HAD ENCOURAGEMENT TO KEEP GOING--
SNIFF
SNIFF

MS. ARTE--
SWAY
SWAY
WHAT IS SHE DOING?
STAND U
PULL

H-HEY! SHE PROMISED ME FIVE MINUTES OF HER TIME!
DRAG

THUD
OUCH!

APHRODITE--

TAKE THIS. YOU'VE BEEN GIVEN SOMETHING NOT MEANT FOR YOUR KIND.
NO! I DON'T TRUST YOU!
SHAKE
SHAKE
TWITCH-
patience
YOU'VE BEEN UNFAIR TO ME. AND NOT ONLY YOU, BUT THE DEMIGODDESSES AROUND YOU, TOO.
I MEAN, IS IT REALLY MY FAULT THAT EROS MISINTERPRETED WHAT I SAID EVERY SINGLE TIME?
THIS LITTLE HUMAN--
NO!!!

APHRODITE--
DON'T KILL HER!
BAM

I'M JUST GIVING HER AN ANTIDOTE TO COUNTERACT THE NECTAR, YOU IDIOTS.
AHH LET ME G
APHRODITE

FWUMP

IT'S THE LEAST I CAN DO SO SHE DOESN'T HUMILIATE HERSELF *MORE* IN FRONT OF HER IDOL.

BUMP
BUMP
BUMP

WANNA HEAD HEAD TO THE TOP? OLYMPIANS-ONLY AFTER-PARTY. NONE OF THOSE BUTT-KISSING DEMIGODS WILL BOTHER US.
MAYBE LATER, DIONYSUS.
I'M SUPPOSED TO MEET SOMEONE NOW....A RATHER INTERESTING HUMAN, I'VE BEEN TOLD.

YOU'VE ALWAYS HAD A SOFT SPOT FOR THE WEIRDEST OF THAT LOT.

WELL, YOUR LOSS, SISTER.

AHH. I'VE FORGOTTEN HOW ANNOYING THEY CAN BE.
sigh
ALTHOUGH... WHERE IS SHE?

THE GIRL THAT THE PAINTER SAID "HAS A SINCERE HEART"?

IS SHE OKAY? HOW DID THIS HAPPEN?! SHE BROUGHT HER OWN FOOD!
WELL, EITHER SHE COULDN'T RESIST OLYMPIAN FARE...OR SOMEONE SLIPPED SOMETHING TO HER.
SHE'S NOT THAT KIND OF PERSON.
SHE'LL BE FINE. NECTAR DOESN'T REALLY MAKE HUMANS DIE. SHE'S JUST VERY, VERY DRUNK.
OH, REALLY?
I WOULDN'T BE SURPRISED IF SHE COULDN'T CONTROL HERSELF.
SIGH
THAT'S ONE OF THE BIGGEST VICES OF HUMANS, AFTER ALL.

IT'S MY FAULT. I'M THE ONE WHO ENCOURAGED HER TO COME.

YOU'RE THE ONE WHO TOLD HER TO COME?! YOU DUMBASS!
GRAB
EVERYONE KNOWS THAT THESE PARTIES ARE NO PLACE FOR A HUMAN!

I WAS JUST TRYING TO SHOW HER THAT SHE'S PART OF OLYMPUS, TOO,
WHETHER SHE'S HUMAN OR NOT. WHICH IS THE OPPOSITE OF WHAT YOU'VE BEEN DOING.
THAT'S NOT THE POINT, MR. HIGH-AND-MIGHTY! HOW WOULD YOU FEEL AT A DINNER PARTY WHERE ANYTHING YOU TOUCH WOULD MAKE YOU DELIRIOUS?
PULL
THAT'S WHY I SAID IT WOULD'VE BEEN MUCH BETTER IF SHE NEVER CAME AT ALL!

YOU SAID THAT SHE CAME PREPARED WITH HER OWN FOOD AND BEVERAGES. THAT MEANS SOMEBODY DID THIS TO HER INTENTIONALLY.
GRAB

OF COURSE YOU'D BELIEVE THAT HUMANS SHOULD NEVER HAVE A PLACE AT THE TABLE.
OH, YOU WANT TO GO THERE?

UGH...
MY HEAD.
BACK OFF, YOU IDIOTS ARE DEPRIVING HER OF OXYGEN.
STOP
HOW IS YOUR HEAD?
UGHH... REALLY DIZZY.
HOW DOES YOUR MOUTH TASTE?
REALLY DRY...
YOU HEARD HER, BOYS. IF ONE OF YOU FEELS LIKE BEING USEFUL, GO GET A BOTTLE OF WATER.
JOLT
HA. LET ME CALL SOMEONE TO--
HOW IS HE SO FAST?!

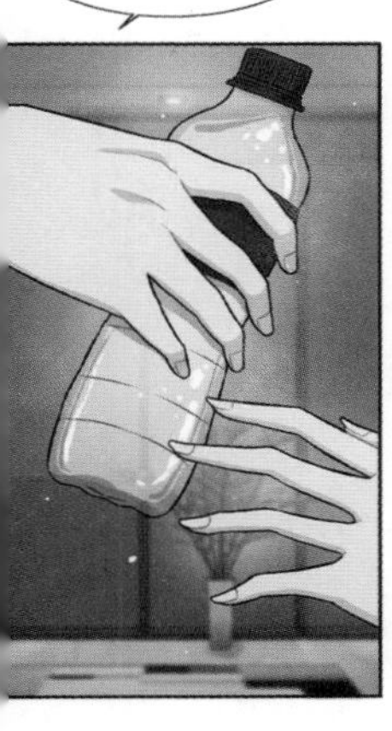
HERE YOU GO.

YOU'RE RIGHT. IT WAS...WRONG OF ME TO INVITE HER TO THIS KIND OF EVENT.

NO SHIT. WHAT CLUED YOU IN ON THAT, GENIUS?

WHEN I GOT BACK TO THE MAIN ROOM, I REALIZED HOW INAPPROPRIATE THE PARTY WAS FOR HUMANS. THE DEMIGODS WERE ALL DRINKING AND TOASTING WITH THE NECTAR...
...AND THE GODS THEMSELVES WERE ABSENT. I'M ASSUMING THEY'VE GONE UP TO THE TOP FLOORS TO HAVE THEIR OWN PARTY.

AND I WAS SUPPOSED TO BE THERE FIVE MINUTES AGO, NOT HERE NURSING THIS INFANT.
GULP
GULP

CLENCH

JUST GET HER HOME.

SLAM

DO YOU KNOW HER ADDRESS?
DO I LOOK LIKE A STALKER TO YOU?
WHY CAN'T YOU JUST ANSWER A SIMPLE YES OR NO QUESTION?
WHY CAN'T YOU BE LESS PRETENTIOUS?
haa...
HAVING A CONVERSATION WITH YOU IS IMPOSSIBLE.
I HAVE HER ADDRESS, SO I'LL TAKE HER HOME.

WHAT?! HOW DO YOU HAVE HER ADDRESS?
JUST... CIRCUMSTANCES.

WELL, I CAN TAKE HER IF YOU TELL ME HER ADDRESS.

NO. I SHOULD DO IT.
I WAS THE ONE WHO INVITED HER. I SHOULD BE THE ONE RESPONSIBLE FOR HER.

GRIT

GRUMBLE
DAMN IT.
RUSTLE

COVER

YOU DON'T HAVE TO DO THAT. I'M GOING STRAIGHT TO THE PARKING LOT. NO ONE'S GOING TO SEE HER LIKE THIS.
SO? SHE STILL LOOKS VERY EXPOSED. AS A VP, IT'S ALSO MY RESPONSIBILITY TO TAKE CARE OF MY SUBORDINATES.

MAKE SURE TO CHECK IN WITH ME ONCE YOU'RE THERE!
I'M GOING NOW.

SEND ME PROOF THAT SHE'S SAFE, OKAY?!

THE COMPANY HAS A ZERO-TOLERANCE POLICY FOR MISCONDUCT!!!

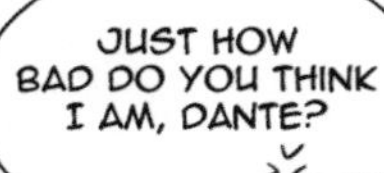

JUST HOW BAD DO YOU THINK I AM, DANTE?

uhh...

hic...
sob...
sob...
sniff sniff
I...
I MISSED MY CHANCE, DIDN'T I? TO MEET ARTEMIS.

IRIS...
SO HOW BAD WAS I?
REACH OUT
YOU WEREN'T THAT BA--
DON'T LIE TO ME, PLEASE.

sniff
sniff
I REMEMBER THAT I...YELLED, A LOT.
I REMEMBER I THREW STUFF AROUND, TOO.

NOBODY CAN BLAME YOU. THEY'LL UNDERSTAND.
STOP

NO, ORION, THEY'LL PITY ME!
HALT

THEY'LL PITY ME AND WRITE IT OFF AS BEING EXPECTED FROM THE "STUPID HUMAN."
EVEN IF THEY NEVER MENTION IT TO ME AFTERWARDS, IT'LL ALWAYS BE AT THE BACK OF THEIR MINDS.
"POOR IRIS. PATHETIC HUMAN. SHE CAN'T EVEN CONTROL HERSELF."
AND SHE SAW ALL OF THAT, DIDN'T SHE? ARTEMIS. JUST LIKE YOU SAW ME HUMILIATE MYSELF.
I DON'T EVEN KNOW IF I CAN GO BACK TO OLYMPUS AFTER THI--
HUG
SHE DIDN'T SEE ANYTHING. I MADE SURE OF IT.

AND YOU'RE GOING TO DO SUCH GREAT WORK NEXT WEEK THAT EVERYBODY WILL FORGET THAT ONCE UPON A TIME,
YOU THREW AN APPLE AT AN OFFICE PARTY.

THEY'LL SEE YOU FOR WHO YOU ARE--A HARDWORKING WOMAN WHO'S DOING HER BEST.
SO YOU HAVE TO COME BACK TO OLYMPUS.
BECAUSE YOU HAVE TO SHOW THEM THAT THEY'RE WRONG ABOUT YOU.

Office Gods

DON'T MISS *OFFICE GODS* VOLUME 2!

WOAH, ARE THESE ALL THE PAST SPECIAL EDITION COVERS?
YES. EVERY 10 YEARS, WE PUBLISH A SPECIAL FEATURE DEDICATED TO ONE OF THE OLYMPIANS.
THIS DECADE, THE FOCUS WILL BE ON ARTEMIS.
ORION'S PAINTING REALLY MADE WAVES! WE'RE THINKING OF FEATURING HIS ARTWORK IN THE HERALD, TOO.
I'M TRYING TO FIGURE OUT WHO ELSE WE'RE MISSING...
THERE ARE 12 OLYMPIANS AND ONLY 9 COVERS. I KNOW ZEUS WILL PROBABLY BE THE LAST.
BUT I'M TRYING TO REMEMBER THE OTHER GOD THAT WE'VE YET TO COVER ASIDE FROM ARTEMIS.
WHO IS IT? THERE'S ARTEMIS, APHRODITE, APOLLO, ARTEMIS...
You just said 'Artemis' twice...

IT'S APHRODITE'S EX-HUSBAND.
!
APHRODITE WAS MARRIED?!
WHEN DID THEY GET DIVORCED? HOW?
IS THERE EVEN SUCH A THING AS DIVORCE BETWEEN GODS?

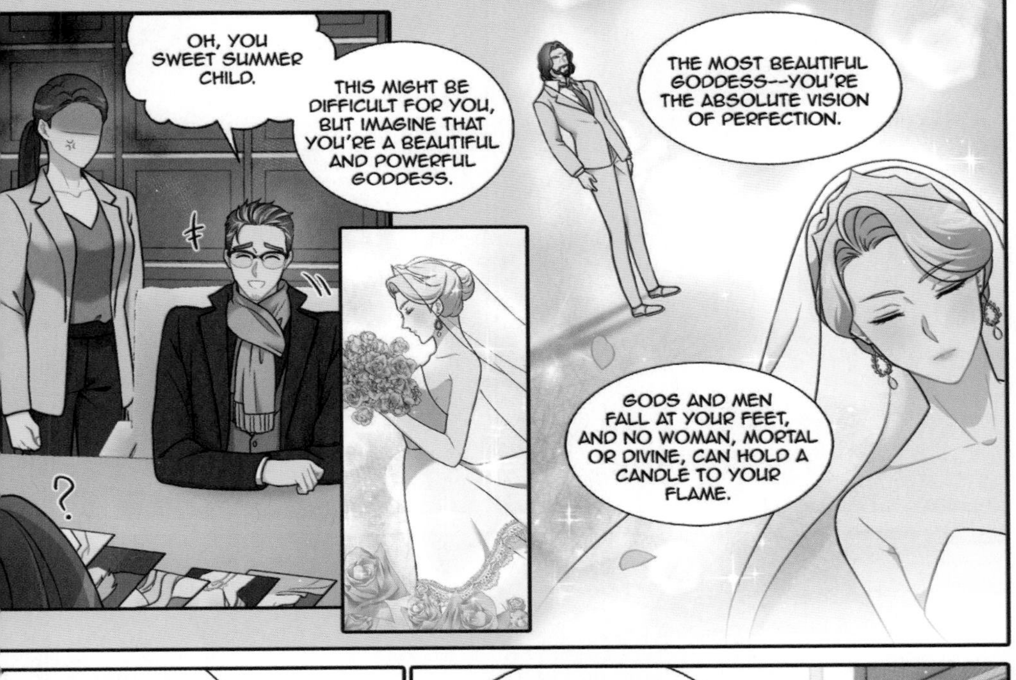
OH, YOU SWEET SUMMER CHILD.
THIS MIGHT BE DIFFICULT FOR YOU, BUT IMAGINE THAT YOU'RE A BEAUTIFUL AND POWERFUL GODDESS.
THE MOST BEAUTIFUL GODDESS--YOU'RE THE ABSOLUTE VISION OF PERFECTION.
GODS AND MEN FALL AT YOUR FEET, AND NO WOMAN, MORTAL OR DIVINE, CAN HOLD A CANDLE TO YOUR FLAME.
?

WHY WOULD YOU EVER SETTLE FOR ANYTHING LESS THAN PERFECTION IN YOUR PARTNER?
?
EVEN THOUGH IT WAS NICE OF APHRODITE TO SET UP ANOTHER CALL FOR ME WITH ARTEMIS, I GUESS HERMES HAS A POINT.
I CAN TOTALLY SEE HER DISMISSING SOMEBODY THAT DOESN'T MEET HER STANDARDS. SHE'S SO...

COLD!

THAT MAY BE FOR THE BEST, THOUGH.
I HEARD THAT HEPHAESTUS NEVER ONCE SMILED DURING HIS SHORT STAY IN OLYMPUS.

TAP
TAP
OH YEAH! HEPHAESTUS!

THAT'S RIGHT. THE ESTEEMED ARCHITECT OF OLYMPUS.

BEFORE LEAVING, HEPHAESTUS DEMANDED THAT WE NEVER ASSOCIATE HIM WITH OLYMPUS AGAIN.
HE SAID THAT OLYMPUS IS THE CREATION HE REGRETS THE MOST.
BUT HONESTLY, MOST OF US THINK HE JUST WANTED TO GET AWAY FROM HIS EX-WIFE...

SPECIAL THANKS

Working on *Office Gods* has been a great joy, and I've learned so much from the process. It's my first time working with so many great minds!

To my editors, Brooke and Wen, thank you for putting up with me and pushing me when it was necessary.

To the Kisai team, thank you for being so professional at handling this.

I'd also like to thank Tapas for the opportunity to work on such an interesting project.

And of course, to my husband Boby, who has always supported me and is my strongest support pillar.

–CAT

ABOUT THE AUTHOR

Despite her penname Demonicblackcat, Cat Octorina is more of a dog person, although she also owns a grumpy black cat that tolerates her presence. She creates comics, and in her spare time, she tries to get better at writing. Once in a blue moon, Cat cooks for her husband and three furbabies. She hopes that this won't be the last time her name is printed inside a book.

ABOUT THE ILLUSTRATOR

Hiikariin always dreamed of becoming a comic artist. One of her greatest influences is Tadatoshi Fujimaki, and once she discovered "Kuroko no Basket," she never looked back. Self-taught, Hiikariin loves and lives to draw.

Andrews McMeel Publishing
a division of Andrews McMeel Universal
1130 Walnut Street, Kansas City, Missouri 64106

www.andrewsmcmeel.com

23 24 25 26 27 SDB 10 9 8 7 6 5 4 3 2 1

ISBN: 978-1-5248-8604-2
Library of Congress Control Number: 2023937023

Book Editor: Betty Wong
Art Director: Holly Swayne
Production Editor: Jasmine Lim
Production Manager: Jeff Preuss
Production Artists: Joamette Gil, Hannah McGill

Studio Tapas
Story: Demonicblackcat
Editors: Brooke Huang & C. Wen Zhang, Qiana Mills
Editor-in-Chief: Gabrielle Luu

In Association with Kisai Entertainment
Art: Hiikariin (additional art by Mea)
Coloring: Fsalmon & Bonob Beneb Studio
Editors: Junjun, Caca Haniyah, Naomi Alf